I0718679

DEFENDING ISABELLA

A STEAMY, SMALL-TOWN PROTECTOR ROMANCE

LYNYRD STATION PROTECTORS - SPECIAL OPS

PJ FIALA

DEDICATION

I've had so many wonderful people come into my life and I want you all to know how much I appreciate it. From each and every reader who takes the time out of their days to read my stories and leave reviews, thank you.
My beautiful, smart and fun PJ Fiala's Road Queens, who play games with me, post fun memes, keep the conversation rolling and help me create these captivating characters, places, businesses and more. Thank you ladies for your ideas, support and love. The following characters and places were created by:
Linda Cooper - Eric Martinez
Kandi Candelas - La quemada
Karen Cranford LeBeau - Carlos Mendoza
Yvonne Cruz (Isabella) Karen Cranford LeBeau (Martinez) - Isabella Martinez
(Diego - Karen Cranford LeBeau) (Josephs - Anna Marie Flamini) - Diego Josephs
Yvonne T. Cruz - Escondito
Marie Evans- Sofia
Jean Fink - Air Quemada

Anna Marie Flamini - Gabriella
Lisa Gibbs - Nueva Laredo
Judy Hamilton - Bianco Martinez
Kristy Hammans Sokol - Cecily Diaz
Melissa Hultz - Tony Morales
Rosa McAnulty - Emiliana Martinez & Ivan Martinez
Kim Ruiz - Meteo Martinez
Christy Seiple - Dominic (Dom) Juarez
Kari Wolff - Magnolia TX

Kerry Harteker - medical questions.
A special thank you to April Bennett -
TheEditingSoprano.com
and Trenda London, my amazing editors!

Last but not least, my family for the love and sacrifices they have made and continue to make to help me achieve this dream, especially my husband and best friend, Gene. Words can never express how much you mean to me. To our veterans and current serving members of our armed forces, police and fire departments and EMTs, thank you ladies and gentlemen for your hard work and sacrifices; it's with gratitude and thankfulness that I mention you in this forward.

DESCRIPTION

GHOST: Government Hidden Ops Specialty Team. They eliminate the threat when no one else can.

GHOST operative Josh Masters loves his life and the excitement of his job. Saying he's married to it, would be accurate. Taking down criminals one by one is the thrill of a lifetime.

Dr. Isabella Martinez will do anything to help others, she's dedicated her life to it. Planning her own clinic while building her medical practice is her passion.

But after her brother disappears, Isabella must enlist the help of the sexy stranger she met at a wedding to locate him before it's too late.

Helping the gorgeous Isabella find her brother is only the start. Unearthing the criminal enterprise her brother founded sends her and her family reeling.

As the kidnappers turn their attention toward Isabella, Josh's new mission is to protect the tantalizing doctor from a predator hellbent on revenge.

Can he do both?

***

Entire series complete!

USA Today bestselling author PJ Fiala brings you the full and complete GHOST series—heroes willing to sacrifice everything in service to their country, and for the women they love. Full length novel with no cliffhanger, no cheating, and a happily-ever-after guaranteed.

***

Let's stay in contact, join my newsletter so I can let you know about new releases, sales, promotions and more. https://www.subscribepage.com/pjfialafm

1

Isabella straightened the bright green tablecloth on one of the forty tables in the enormous backyard of her family's home. She turned at the sound of a large vehicle as it rolled down the driveway.

A bus which, upon closer inspection, was the same bus her brother Eric had left on last night for his bachelor party, pulled close to the house, and her stomach turned over. This was not good. He should have been home hours ago.

Emiliana, Isabella's younger sister, walked to Isabella's side.

"This is trouble, Isi."

"I was just thinking the same thing. Where is Mamá?"

Both sisters turned toward the back doors perched atop a palatial stone patio to see their mother as she stepped out of the house and onto the patio. The worry that marred Bianca's beautiful face confirmed their suspicions; mamá expected trouble too.

The door to the bus opened and out stepped a group of men, most of them wobbling on their feet, with silly grins on their faces and their clothing in varying degrees of disarray.

Finally, after several unknown men had stepped off the bus, a tall, broad-shouldered man exited the bus half carrying Eric.

The back door of the Martinez's family home opened and then slammed shut. Isabella's shoulders rose to her ears as she feared the glass on the custom oak door would shatter at the impact.

Eric's future bride...nope, Eric's very *angry* bride, Cecily Diaz, was not yet in her wedding dress but wearing a white, silken robe; her shiny, dark hair was perfectly coifed for her wedding ceremony, without the veil, her makeup impeccable, her tawny-colored legs peeking from the slit in the robe approached Eric.

With each long stride she took toward her future husband--if he lived that long--she marched toward the group of men.

If the situation weren't so serious, her white tennis shoes would have looked almost comical under the silk of her robe. "There she is boys..." Eric slurred. "My beautiful bride," he managed to get out before Cecily let him have it.

Her fists were balled tightly at her sides and Isabella worried that she'd be patching up her brother before he made it to the altar today.

"You must have a death wish Eric Martinez." Cecily kept her voice low, but her ire lent steel to her words. "How dare you, on this day, our wedding day, disgrace me and my family, as well as your own, by staying out all night, drinking and doing Lord knows what else, only to show up for the ceremony four hours beforehand drunk out of your mind."

Isabella walked forward, her sister Emiliana close behind her. "Cecily, let me take him in and get him cleaned up. It'll be all right."

"It won't be all right. Not now. He's ruined my perfect day. The day I've planned my ass off for. My parents, your parents, everyone has been working on this wedding for a year." Cecily skewered Eric with a glare. "A fucking year!"

Isabella turned to her sister. "Emi, take Cecily back inside and let me deal with Eric."

Emi hesitantly approached Cecily. "Ceci, let's go and finish getting ready. Isi will take care of Eric. I promise it'll be all right."

Emi looked at her over Cecily's shoulder, hoping for an encouraging nod. Isabella gave it to her and sent up silent prayers that she could sober up her stupid brother before the ceremony. It wasn't going to be easy though.

She approached Eric as the men either disbursed or climbed back on the bus. She didn't know many of these men, which didn't surprise her since she'd lived in Texas for the past ten years, first finishing medical school, then practicing at The Medical Clinic in Magnolia just outside of Galveston.

The man holding Eric up chuckled and said, "Why don't you point me in the direction where you want him and I'll get him there for you. He's not very good on his feet right now."

"Why would you let him drink so much?"

"Look, Princess, I had nothing to do with how much he drank. He was well on his way when I met him a few hours ago."

"You mean you just met him?"

"A few hours ago. He was celebrating pretty hard."

Shaking her head, she walked to the right side of Eric,

put her arm around his waist and tried hefting Eric off the big man hanging on to him. When she nearly dropped to her knees at Eric's weight, he looked over her brother's head at her and said, "Just point. I'll follow."

Taking a deep breath, she looked up to see Cecily standing on the patio watching them, and Emi trying her hardest to get Cecily inside. Thinking it best to look like this would be doable, Isabella said, "Fine. Let's go in the side door, I'm afraid Cecily will stab him in the gut if he gets too close right now."

The larger man looked up at Cecily, then nodded. "Yep. She looks pretty pissed off."

He started walking with Eric stumbling alongside him and Isabella shook her head while she made a mental inventory of the supplies she'd need to try and sober her brother up.

Cecily took two steps toward them as they walked past to the side door. "And another thing, asshole, you won't be touching this..." She flung her robe open, showing off her beautiful white lace teddy she'd purchased just for this night. "At all."

Emi grabbed the robe and pulled it closed, but Eric chose that moment to try and whistle. "Whoop, hot mamá, here I come."

"Fucker." Cecily yelled just as Emi and her mamá ushered her inside the house.

"Bud, you need to let her cool down before trying to be...whatever that was." The large man said to her brother.

Isabella looked over at him and half smiled. At least he was smart enough to know that much and sober enough to practically carry her dumbass brother.

"My name's Josh."

Hesitating briefly before responding, "Isabella."

"Is he normally a partier?"

"Not like this. My other brother, Mateo, is the partier."

She turned then; her brows bunched together. "Was Mateo with all of you?"

Josh turned and looked at the bus and the few men still talking and laughing by the front of it.

"Hm, I don't recall a Mateo. But, honestly, we only met this group a few hours ago."

Isabella stopped and stared in disbelief at him.

"I can't believe you didn't know these guys you were partying with."

He shrugged, his smile stretching across his handsome face; his perfect teeth were white, his lips full, his blue dress-shirt unbuttoned to the third button, giving her a hint of firm muscled chest.

"I know my friends, Diego, Travis and Shep."

Isabella crossed her arms over her chest.

"Where did you meet my brother and his friends?"

"El Paso."

"Texas?" She almost yelled.

His head jerked back a bit. "Yes, ma'am."

"So, let me get this straight. You met up with and drank with a group of men you didn't know. Then climbed on a bus and crossed the border into another country with them."

He took a deep breath and his impressive chest rose and fell. The weight of her brother, who was now almost dead weight and dozing, seemed like nothing to him. "Look, I'm just in Texas to celebrate my friend Travis's bachelor party. He's getting married next weekend and I'm here for the week. We went out, met Eric and his friends, had a great time. Most of them are great guys and we had fun. Eric insisted we come to his wedding and since I was the most sober one, I wanted to make sure he made it back in time. Between you and me, some of his friends aren't the best influence."

"No kidding."

She shot a look back at the motley group and wondered where her father was because he'd be out to whip ass soon. Just as the thought occurred to her, he stepped out onto the patio, and Isabella picked up her pace as they rounded the patio on the lower level to get Eric inside before Papa chewed him out.

She could hear her father's voice as he barked out orders to the men standing around, some of them staying here in the guest house, telling them to get themselves cleaned up and stop behaving like idiots or there'd be hell to pay.

She opened the side door, which entered into the lower level of her parents' home and walked quickly down the hall where the guest bedrooms were housed along with Eric's. Her bedroom was upstairs where she'd spent most of her lifetime.

2

———

Josh mostly carried Eric down the hallway in the spectacular home of the Martinez family, until Isabella opened a door on the left, about halfway down, to a spacious earth-toned bedroom. The king-sized bed against the left wall was covered in a comforter of muted earth tones and beautiful pottery pieces were hung or situated throughout the room.

He lay Eric on the bed, looked around for a waste-basket and brought it to the bed.

"Do you need me to get him in the shower?"

He looked over at Isabella, the gorgeous sister of his new drunk friend, and tried remembering meeting someone as beautiful as she was. Ever. In his entire life. He couldn't.

She disappeared behind a door and he heard a shower turn on. Returning to the bedroom, she looked at him and his heartbeat sped up. Her dark, hair shone in the sunlight streaming through the windows. She had half of it pulled up on the top of her head in some twisted style. Her eyes, dark as coal, sparkled and her full lips glistened.

He wanted to taste them. Touch her. Know her. She held herself straight and tall, though he guessed her to only be around 5'2" or so. Her skin was the perfect blend of olive and cream, so clear and smooth. She was breathtaking.

She made a quick assessment of the situation, looked at her watch and sighed.

"Why don't you get him in the shower; I'll go upstairs and get my bag."

He watched her exit and told himself she might just be way out of his league, but he wanted to know how far. He didn't grow up in a place like this, though he lived in a place similar to this one now.

Taking a deep breath, he looked at Eric, who was watching him, a goofy grin on his face.

"She's not gonna bite on your hook, man. She wants nothing to do with this place or anything in it."

"I'm not in this place."

Eric chuckled.

"All right, Bud, let's get you in the shower."

He reached down to pull his drunk friend up, only to have Eric rollover. "Naw, I'll just sleep for a bit."

Taking a deep breath and settling in for a fight, Josh walked around the bed and with one quick jerk, grabbed Eric's hand and pulled him up, bent and put his shoulder to Eric's stomach, then threw him over his shoulder and quickly carried him to the bathroom.

Opening the door of the bathroom, the steam rolled out in billows but Josh forged ahead. He stopped at the large vanity, and propped Eric against the edge as he pulled his wallet and phone out of his pocket. Lifting his left leg, he unstrapped his ankle holster and lay it and his gun on the vanity along with his watch. He then turned and opened the shower door and dragged Eric inside.

Getting drenched himself, he grabbed the shampoo bottle on the ledge, squeezed some in his hand and began washing Eric's dark hair, much like his sister's.

Eric sputtered under the water but stopped when he sucked in a mouthful of water that tasted of shampoo, choking and coughing, while Josh did his best to help his friend sober up. Throwing up some of that alcohol was probably a good thing.

Dunking Eric under the warm spray of water once more, he waited until all the soap washed from Eric's hair, then pulled him back out. The large shower had a bench at the back, so Josh sat Eric on the bench, turned off the water, then stepped out, dripping water everywhere, and went in search of towels.

Finding a cabinet alongside the shower, he pulled a stack from the cabinet, laid one on the floor, then began unbuttoning Eric's shirt. The limp man rested his head against the shower. Though it was tedious and difficult getting Eric's clothing off, he managed, all except his underwear. He had no intention of taking off another man's underwear.

Taking one of the soft, white towels, he dried Eric's hair, then wrapped the towel over his shoulders, pulled him to his unsteady feet and wrapped a towel around his waist.

Wrapping himself in towels so he didn't get everything sopping wet, he managed to get Eric out of the bathroom without slipping only to find Isabella sitting on the edge of the bed with medical supplies lying about.

Isabella stood up. Her eyes landed on his, then swooped down his body, and it was as if he could feel her touching him. She smoldered. He smoldered.

Eric wobbled and Josh got him to the bed and laid him

down. He began sopping some of the water from his clothing as he watched Isabella tie a rubber band around Eric's upper arm.

"What are you doing?"

"I'm giving him an IV to try and sober him up."

"How do you know to do that?"

She never looked away from what she was doing as she hooked an IV to the top of the headboard of the bed, pulled some tape from a portable dispenser and stuck it to her forearm.

She inserted the needle into Eric's vein, taped the needle in place, adjusted the amount of fluid going into him, then answered, "I'm a physician in Texas, where I live."

Holy shit, stunning and smart. Lethal.

"Is that going to work?"

"It's the only remedy there is for alcohol over-consumption."

Josh chuckled.

Isabella pulled a bottle of water off the nightstand and walked to where he stood. She looked down his body, then at the puddle of water on the stone floors.

"If you want to go to the bathroom and take your clothes off, I'll go see if I can find something you can wear until your clothes dry."

She left the room without waiting for an answer so he shrugged, walked back to the bathroom, and closed and locked the door.

Taking his clothes off, he thought he may as well duck back into the shower and clean up properly; it would save him time later, since they were due back at the wedding in less than four hours. He initially hadn't been all that excited about going to two weddings this week, but now that he'd met Isabella, he was eager to come back, under better circumstances, and see if he could get to know her better.

He showered quickly, and exited the shower, using another of the towels he'd pulled out previously.

Towel drying his body and hair, he wrapped the towel around his waist, and unlocked and opened the door slightly. A stack of clothing lay on a chair pulled next to the door, but Isabella was not in the room. A bit sad he couldn't look at her again, he grabbed the clothing and dressed in the bathroom. He'd be commando until he got back to his hotel in Texas, but he'd done that before. Missions didn't always go as you expected, and improvisation was an all-important skill in his line of work.

The expensive dress slacks, socks and shirt were slightly too large for him, but he'd make it work. He'd be sitting on a bus most of the way back to the hotel anyway.

Strapping his gun on his ankle, dropping his wallet in a back pocket, his phone into his front right pocket and reattaching his watch, Josh opened the door again to see Isabella sitting on the edge of the bed taking her brother's pulse.

The puddle he'd made in the floor was gone. "Thank you for cleaning up the water on the floor."

"I didn't do it. Elisa did."

"Okay. Thank you to Elisa then."

Isabella stood and faced him; her arms crossed over her chest. "How is it you aren't that drunk?"

"Self-control."

She shrugged. "Do you know what he was drinking?"

"His friends were lining up the shots. I have no idea what was in them."

"Stupid." She looked at her brother once more then at her watch.

"How is the bride doing?"

"My sister, Emiliana, is calming her down. She's a bit of a firecracker, but she'll cool down. She and Eric are perfect for each other and they'll work through this."

He nodded. "Okay, well if you don't have anything else you need me to do, I'd better get going or the bus will leave without me."

He stepped toward the door then stopped. "I do remember Mateo. He was there earlier but left with some friends."

3

"Thanks, I'll let Papa know."

Mateo, she was so tired of always worrying about Mateo. Her whole life seemed to revolve around Mateo. Where was he? How did he get wherever he was? Who was he with? When would he come home or straighten up or whatever plethora of troublesome questions that concerned Mateo. He was the bad seed. Yet she and her siblings had to pay for Mateo's actions by always being tasked with keeping watch over him. It was the main reason she moved to the United States, got her education, got her citizenship, then got a position practicing medicine at The Medical Clinic in Magnolia, Texas.

She watched Josh's face as he assessed her. He was good though; she couldn't tell what he was thinking. She sure as hell didn't need his distraction right now either. She just needed to get Eric married then get home and resume her life. Without drama. And without this sexy beast before her messing with her head. Even if he was built, lean but built. Smart. Sexy. He was the trifecta.

He stared for a while longer and she couldn't look

away from him. His eyes were similar to hers in color, dark brown framed in thick, dark lashes. His coloring was slightly lighter than hers, but he was certainly of Hispanic heritage.

Finally, he turned, and her eyes landed on his fine backside, dressed in her father's clothing. Her father had gained some weight in recent years, which showed now in the clothing as Josh wore them. They hung on him a bit, but he still filled them out nicely.

The door slowly closed, and she stared at it for a while before turning to her brother and wondering how long she should let him sleep. Likely another hour or two, then the fun would begin. For now, she'd go in search of Cecily and see if Emiliana had managed to calm her down. Taking in a deep breath, she eased herself out of Eric's bedroom and down the hall.

The sound of the bus pulling out of the driveway reached her ears and she felt a tiny bit sad, but then again, relieved. Maybe he wouldn't come to the wedding and further distract her. Lord knew she had enough to deal with.

She walked up the staircase to the main floor common area between the kitchen and living room. Dishes clattered in the kitchen as the catering staff they'd hired for today busily prepared the food for the reception, which her parents graciously agreed to host. Cecily's family had become close friends of the family and while they were not poor, they didn't have the wealth that her parents had amassed. This home, which had been her father's parents' before his, had been beautifully redecorated under the artistic eye of her mother. Isabella's father, Ivan, was a very astute businessman with a diverse portfolio of businesses that ranged from nursing homes to laundromats to a car dealership. Eric now worked with their father in his business, learning to run the business one day.

Turning to the left, she found her mother standing at a large bank of windows, looking out on the expanse of lawn that was currently being transformed into a wedding venue complete with a white carpet and padded folding chairs for the guests. An ornate pergola had been constructed over the past two weeks and it was currently being decorated with white flowers of various types and yards of gossamer covered mini lights. It was going to be a gorgeous wedding, despite the groom's earlier lack of decorum.

"Mamá, everything is looking beautiful."

Her mother turned to her, a mature version of herself, her weak smile spoke her true sadness. "Thank you, querida. Now how is your brother doing?"

"I'm pumping fluids through him by IV. Currently he's sleeping. The tiredness doesn't help. I'll wake him in an hour or two and make him drink a few bottles of water. It's all we can do at this point."

Her mother wrapped her left arm around Isabella's waist and pulled her close.

"These boys have aged me three times my age. It's always something with them."

"Yes, Mamá."

Isabella lay her head on her mother's shoulder and stood transfixed as the artisans outside created a wedding wonderland. Her mother always made her feel better.

"Has anyone heard from Mateo?"

Taking a deep breath Isabella responded. "Josh said he saw Mateo last night, but he left early."

"Josh. Is that the handsome man who helped you with Eric?"

"Yes."

"Hmm."

"Don't get any ideas, Mamá. He's handsome, but that's where it ends. I don't need a distraction. I'm just inches away from starting my own medical clinic and I don't want any complications."

"You can have both, querida."

Isabella stood straight. "Let's focus on getting my drunk brother sober enough to marry the love of his life. Then getting my wayward brother home, ready for the wedding and out of trouble for a while."

Kissing her mother on the cheek, she ascended the stairs leading to the bedrooms, where Cecily was getting ready in Emi's longtime bedroom, and Emiliana was helping her.

Knocking on Emi's door, she twisted the knob and inched it open.

"May I come in?"

Emiliana waved her in. "Yes, come in."

Cecily sat in a chair, her eyes red-rimmed from crying, while a nail tech painted her fingernails a pearly white adding tiny rhinestones to the tips in various places. Isabella looked over the nail tech's shoulders at the beautiful job she was doing then winked at Cecily.

"What a beautiful bride you are, Ceci."

Ceci took a deep breath and smiled. "How is my sassy husband-to-be?"

"He's resting now, and I have an IV in his arm pushing fluids in. We'll have him as right as we can and if I know my younger brother, he'll spend the rest of his life making this up to you. According to Josh, some of his friends are a bad influence and had shots lined up all night. I'm sure when asked, he will say he never meant to get so drunk. I know for a fact he'll tell you he never meant to hurt you. You are his heart."

A lone tear fell down Ceci's cheek. "Thank you." She sniffed daintily. "I'm still pissed off though."

"Yep. I would be, too."

Isabella turned to her sister, who sat in a chair by the window, her hands on her lap. Picking up her sister's hands, Isabella looked at her beautifully shaped and polished nails, in soft pink.

"Stunning."

"Are you sure you don't want your nails done, Isi?"

"I'm sure. It's a shame to spend the time and money when I'd have to take it all off tomorrow anyway. I can't wear such things at work."

Emi's face scrunched as she frowned. "I'm glad I went into graphic design."

Isabella laughed. "And you should perfectly understand not spending the money for such a short amount of time."

A soft knock on the door caused her to turn her head. Elisa, the Martinez's housekeeper peered around the door.

"Ms. Isabella, Eric is awake and creating a fuss about being thirsty."

She smiled. "That's a good sign."

4

───────

The bus ride back to the hotel across the border in Texas seemed bumpier than the ride to the Martinez's place. But then again, he was tired before and slept most of the way. Actually, they all did. When he'd finally climbed aboard the bus, his friends were all strewn about the rented vehicle sleeping. He found himself a spot close to the front, and he now wondered if he should have gone to the back.

The bus slowed and he opened his eyes to see they were about to turn into the hotel parking lot. He sat up and rubbed his eyes as the bus turned in and parked. The driver opened the door and smiled as they exited.

"I will be here at eleven o'clock to pick you all up."

Josh stopped and looked him in the eye. "You're taking us to the wedding?"

"Yes, sir. Mr. Martinez insisted and has already paid for your trip."

Nodding, he smiled and waved. "Thank you, see you at eleven."

He walked to the doors of the hotel, his friends Diego,

Travis and Shep slowly falling in behind him. He'd known these guys for years. They'd served in the military together and stayed in touch, despite Josh's crazy schedule. Travis was now a dentist and getting married next weekend. Josh made a mental note not to let Travis go out the night before. Diego was a convenience store owner, though he'd sell it in a heartbeat for something security-related if he thought he could do it; his PTSD still tormented him. And Shep owned a bike shop. Josh was the only one to keep a military type of business. And truth be told, he felt a bit like a liar, because his friends didn't really know what he actually did for a living other than security.

They entered the elevator, each of them tired and, his friends more than him, still a tad drunk. Josh never drank that much and it served him well last night. He had an ever watchful and always "on duty" mindset; it was difficult to let it go. He'd been an operative...things go sideways to risk having one too many drinks.. Plus, GHOST was in his blood. His father and late brother, Jake, had been operatives at GHOST. His father by example and Jake by his words and actions had taught him and his sister, Jax, the importance and seriousness of their work, the pride to take in doing it, and the responsibility to his co-operatives to have their backs.

The elevator stopped on their floor and they each walked to their rooms, which were in a row.

"Later guys. Bus will be here at eleven." Josh called.

"Yo." Shep called, and no one else said a word.

Flopping on the bed to settle in, he promptly jumped up, remembering he was wearing someone else's clothes. Tiredly walking to the bathroom, Josh carefully removed the clothes he wore and folded them neatly in a pile and lay them on the dresser in his room. He'd take them back with him, though he felt bad he didn't have Mrs. James here to wash them first.

Too tired to worry about it, he lay his gun on the nightstand, his phone alongside it and his wallet next to his phone. He flopped on the bed once more, set his alarm on his phone for 10:00 and closed his eyes to get a few moments of sleep.

———

The bus wove down the long driveway and Josh spent a few moments enjoying the view. The estate was huge, sprawling over many acres of lush trees and green lawns. The entire blacktopped driveway, which he estimated to be close to a mile long, was lined with white posts and green and pink ribbons tied to the top of them, the tails blowing in the light breeze.

As the home came into view the transformation from this morning till now was unbelievable.

"Whoa, this is amazing." Diego said.

Each of his friends were looking through the front windows of the bus, a smaller one than this morning, but still much too large for just the four of them.

Travis, the groom of their group, muttered, "I'm glad Julie isn't looking at this. Our wedding won't be so grand as this one, that's a fact."

Josh laughed along with his friends.

"Okay, guys, how about we look and act like good guests and not get hammered tonight?"

Shep nudged him on the shoulder. "Trying to impress the gorgeous sister?"

"It's not that."

His friends laughed.

"It so is." Diego laughed.

"It's not, I just..."

His eyes spotted Isabella walking across the lawn to the pergola carrying a book—a Bible, that's what it was—and gently laying it on the podium. She turned at the sound of the bus and he felt as if she were looking in at him. His cheeks heated and his stomach felt like there were bees buzzing around inside.

Diego laughed again. "Look at that boys. Josh is about as red as my shirt."

He glanced at his friend. The mirth in his eyes was a far cry from the usual sadness that haunted Diego's gaze.

Shaking his head, he ignored his friends and their teasing. Josh peered out the bus window again and Isabella was gone. He brushed off a moment of sadness; of course she was still here, and he'd absolutely spend some time talking to her tonight. She was like a magnet.

He quickly shook his head to remove the thought, it was stupid to think such things. She'd sort of given him the idea that she was not interested; and even in his drunken state, hadn't Eric said as much?

Straightening his white dress shirt and black slacks as he stood, Josh picked up his sport coat and adjusted his tie. He grabbed the handle of the white paper bag from the hotel in which he'd placed his borrowed clothes and stepped off the bus last. His friends had begun to walk ahead of him, talking quietly among themselves and Josh sent up a silent prayer that all would be good today. Eric's bride seemed rather unhappy with him earlier.

As they neared the seating area, where a few guests had already found seats, Josh looked at his friends and nodded to an empty chair.

"Save me a seat, I'm going to find someone to take care of these clothes."

Travis smiled, "Of course you are."

He turned and saw Isabella standing at the end of the patio watching him, and his heart hammered in his chest. As he walked toward her, he chastised himself for acting the fool. She had no interest, and he shouldn't either. He'd be going back to Texas today and then be gone in a week.

5

She had intended to pop out and see if most of the guests were seated. They had fifteen minutes until the wedding began and she was grateful Eric was up and somewhat functional. Cecily came down to talk to him a while ago and Isabella waited in the hall in case there were problems. She was still extremely irritated with him, but she left at least somewhat happy that he was getting himself straightened out. Apparently, Eric had apologized profusely and from what she gathered from Eric's end of the conversation, there was jewelry promised.

Her eyes landed on Josh and his friends as they walked to the white padded seats. His friends sat in the back row, and Josh pointed to a seat then turned and was now walking toward her. Her good sense told her to walk back inside, but she wanted to see if he was still as sexy as she'd thought or if it was the fact that his wet shirt clung to his abs showed her that he worked out. Hard. There was certainly something about a man who took care of himself. He likely had the stamina of a...

"Hello again. You look gorgeous."

His scent floated to her and goosebumps formed on her arms. Damn he smelled amazing. His eyes were bright and shiny, his smile was drool worthy and he looked very attractive in his suit.

"Ah, thank you. You look very handsome."

He smiled at her and her foolish knees got weak.

"I brought back the clothes you loaned me. I wasn't sure who I should give them to, and I apologize that I had no way to get them washed before coming back. Please forgive me."

She reached out and took the bag from his hand but wasn't able to avoid touching him. She certainly felt the shock as his fingers lingered. His nostrils flared and she saw him swallow, so apparently he felt it too.

She took a deep breath. "You're forgiven and thank you for bringing them back. I didn't tell Papa that I borrowed them from his closet, so I'll just ask Elisa to wash them and put them away. No one will be the wiser."

"Is this Josh?" Her mother's voice sounded from behind her.

She swallowed and turned to look at her mother.

"Yes, this is Josh. Josh, my mother, Bianca Martinez."

Her mother, graceful and beautiful as ever stepped forward and held her hand out for Josh to shake. As soon as he took her hand, she smiled her brightest smile, which caused him to smile just as large and it was breathtaking.

"It's nice to meet you, Mrs. Martinez. And it's Masters, Josh Masters."

"Thank you so much for making sure our Eric made it home safely."

"You're welcome, Mrs. Martinez. Glad to be of assistance."

Her mother nodded then looked out over the crowd.

"We'll be starting soon but I hope you'll be here for the reception, Josh. Isabella can show you around the estate if you'd like. We have gorgeous Koi ponds, extensive flower gardens and many interesting things to explore here."

She knew her mother was going to push this. Josh smiled brightly, then his eyes landed on hers and she got those goosebumps again.

"I'd love a private tour if you don't mind, Isabella."

The way her name flowed from his mouth made her want to hear it again and again.

"Of course, I don't mind."

She smiled brightly, then stepped back, "Well, I'd better get this inside to Elisa and check on Eric one last time."

She heard Josh tell her mother how gorgeous everything was before taking his seat so she could attend to last minute details. Her mother cooed. For goodness' sake, he was handsome, built, and seemed responsible...but so was her father.

Tossing her head slightly, she walked through the kitchens and into a back area of the house, close to her father's office where Elisa also had an office. She kept track of many of the household and lawn care schedules there and it gave her a place to have a quiet moment when she needed it.

"Elisa, the man who helped Eric home brought these clothes back. I loaned them to him and didn't tell Papa. Will you be able to have them laundered and put back in his closet?"

"Of course, Ms. Isabella."

The sweet woman, who had been employed by her family for three decades now, smiled as she took the bag.

"Thank you."

As Isabella left to see to her brother she met Cecily coming down the stairs in her wedding gown. "Oh, my goodness, Ceci. You are radiant."

Pride filled her that her brother was getting to marry the woman of his dreams and everything from this point forward would be perfect for their day. Ceci beamed.

"Thank you." She looked down the basement stairs. "Is Eric ready?"

"I'm going down to check on him now. He was close to it when I left him down there just a few minutes ago."

Ceci nodded. Emiliana, who'd followed Ceci down the stairs, winked at her, and Isi's stomach settled a bit. She took her sister's hand and squeezed as she walked past, receiving a reassuring squeeze in return.

Just as she started down the stairs, Mateo came running down from the second level. Isabella stopped to look at him; he had a black-eye.

"Mateo, what on earth happened to you?"

"Never mind, Sissy. Go and get Eric so he isn't late after this morning. We'll talk later."

Mateo brushed past her with haste, quickly skirted Ceci and Emi and blew out the patio doors. She watched until his head disappeared down the outside steps; her eyes caught Emi's, both worried now that Mateo was involved in something again. It never ended with him and when it did, it was never well.

6

The bridesmaids walked down the aisle with smiles on their faces, likely relieved that this wedding was actually happening. The final bridesmaid was Isabella. Before the bridesmaids had started down the aisle, Josh briefly had glanced at the altar where the ushers stood waiting for the bridesmaids. He then looked at the best man. Mateo, who he recognized from last night, was sporting a black eye and a couple of cuts and bruises on his face.

Josh's eyes hadn't left Isabella for more than a few seconds. Isabella looked at him as she approached, and his heartbeat increased. There was something about this smart beauty that revved his engines every time he saw her. At almost forty-one years old, he'd never experienced this feeling before. Must be getting old or something.

Isabella passed by. She walked like royalty, her shoulders pulled back, her posture impeccable. Tendrils of her dark hair brushed the exposed skin of her back and his fingers tingled with the desire to do the same.

"Ridiculous," he mumbled to himself.

The music volume increased, and the bride, Cecily, and her father walked down the patio steps and toward the aisle. All the guests stood, but his eye was on Isabella. She smiled when Cecily neared her, and when Cecily handed her the bouquet, Isabella winked. These ladies were already like sisters.

Eric looked upon his bride with pride, maybe a little fear, but it was clear in his smile that he thought she was beautiful. And she was. Her hair wasn't as dark as the Martinez family's, her coloring a tad lighter. But she was a beauty. The Martinez family was a stunning family, and the pictures would be amazing.

Josh remembered the last family picture the Masters had taken. He was sixteen when his father was killed, and the family photo was just four months before. His brother Jake was killed at the farm of Skye Winter's parents while he was on a mission. His parents were so in love and they showered their children with love. The only one who rebelled was his twin sister, Jacqueline, Jax. She'd wanted to be a soldier from the time she was very little, even before Josh wanted to be one. When their father joined the fledgling GHOST after Auggie's daughter, Keirnan, was kidnapped, Jax was so excited. When their father came home, she would sit next to him and ask all the questions. Where had he gone? What had he done? Did he have to kill someone? Why did they set up operations the way they did? She wanted all the details. Then she'd sit in her room and draw out what the operation looked like in her mind. She'd been a tactical operative even back then. Now she was the mother of twins of her own and still an operative.

During the Mass when it came time for the vows between Cecily and Eric to be exchanged, there were tears and smiles everywhere. Although he knew he should be participating in the Mass as it continued, Josh sat in the sun, surrounded by all the beauty of the grounds, lost in thoughts of his family. There had been so many times over the years he'd missed his father. But his older brother Jake had been there to pick up the slack. Until he went into the service. Josh and Jax soon followed and then they'd followed Jake to GHOST. It seemed perfect, working and living with his siblings.

The guests stood as Father Diaz gave the blessing to all of the attendees. Then the recession song started and Eric and Cecily began walking down the aisle toward them. Eric looked at him as he neared, stopped and shook his hand.

"Thanks for saving my ass, man." he whispered.

Josh smiled and shook his head. "Just being a good human, man. Looks like you saved your own ass."

They continued on and Josh turned his head to see Isabella and Mateo approaching. Their eyes met, held and his breath caught.

Diego bumped him and whispered, "She's got it for you, man."

"I don't think so, Diego. She's not interested from what I hear."

"A woman doesn't look like that at a man unless she's interested."

Emiliana and her groomsman and the rest of the bridal party, six couples in all, passed by and the ushers started leading the family members out first.

Bianca and Ivan came next and Bianca stopped when they neared.

"Ivan, this is the man who made sure our Eric made it

home safe and sound. Josh Masters, this is my husband, Ivan."

Josh held his hand out, "Pleasure to meet you, Mr. Martinez."

"The pleasure is mine and thank you for getting Eric home. We are eternally grateful."

Bianca then winked at him, and they walked past him.

Diego elbowed him and snickered, but Josh ignored him. He'd be gone in a week, and he'd do well to remember that fact.

By the time they were excused, he was ready for something to eat; he hadn't had anything except a meal bar and the heat made him slightly tired. Well, that and the fact that he hadn't slept more than three hours in the past day.

They walked through the procession line and offered the bride and groom their congratulations. Eric shook his hand and held it.

"Cecily, this is Josh, I mentioned him this morning."

"Hi, Josh, Emi was chattering about you this morning. Thank you for your help."

"No problem."

He eagerly walked on, shook Mateo's hand, and then shook Isabella's hand and held on. It was electrifying. He could actually feel a current running between them. She pulled away abruptly and he masked his disappointment by turning to the next groomsman and Emiliana and then down the line.

Josh and his friends walked over to the hors d'oeuvres table and filled plates to sate--or at least partially sate--their appetites.

"You want a drink, man?" Diego asked.

"Only water right now."

"Got it."

Diego came back to a table where they sat to eat with four bottles of water with the Martinez name on them. It looked like Mr. Martinez was also in the water business.

A soft hand on his shoulder surprised him and he turned his head; Bianca Martinez smiled.

"Josh, would you mind coming with me for a moment?"

7

Laughing at a joke her Uncle Hector made, Isabella turned her head and saw Mamá walking with Josh toward the house. She watched as they disappeared into the side doors by the den and then found that she couldn't stop watching after they left. She shouldn't care. But she did.

"Excuse me, Uncle Hector, I'll be around soon. I have a few hellos to say."

"Of course, of course. I'm sure we'll be here."

Walking toward the house, she couldn't help but look around at the guests. Everyone was enjoying themselves. Poor Eric, though he deserved it, looked happy but tired and Ceci wasn't letting him sit for a moment; he was going to pay for last night by being forced to endure the nonstop handshaking and congratulations by every distant relative from here to the other side of the world. Smiling at his punishment, she had to give Ceci credit. It was a great punishment.

As she neared the steps to the patio, she glanced over and saw Mateo on the phone, alongside the wall of the house. His brows were pinched together, and the tone of his voice and set of his jaw told her this was not a good phone call. The ever-present question of what he'd gotten himself into this time flitted through her mind, but she was tired of Mateo's problems and she was determined to avoid them while she was home this time. Tomorrow morning she'd go back to Magnolia.

She ascended the five steps that took her to the patio. Just as she reached for the handle to open the door, Josh stepped out and bumped into her. Literally.

Isabella tried stepping back, determined not to fall, "I'm sorry."

He caught her by grabbing her upper arms. The smile on his face was mesmerizing. "No need to be sorry."

The strength with which he easily held her, and the solidness of his stance, was impressive.

Righting herself, she felt her cheeks heat and her heart race. She cleared her throat and tried getting her thoughts together as her mother and father stepped out onto the patio with them.

"Isi, why don't you show Josh around the grounds now?" her mother asked.

She'd been avoiding this. It's why she stayed across the lawn most of the afternoon.

She looked into his eyes. They were gorgeous brown eyes, and he didn't blink as he stared back at her. "Are you sure that won't be too boring for you, Josh?"

"Oh, not at all, I think it will be most enjoyable." He smiled again and she felt as though he was teasing her. Her eyes darted to her parents who both smiled as if they had a secret, and since they'd just had some sort of secret meeting she felt like she'd been left out of it.

Turning she started walking toward the steps, but she

could feel his presence behind her. She could still smell his cologne. She could still feel his hands on her arms.

At the bottom step she turned to him. "Would you like to see the Koi ponds first or the athletic courts?"

"Either is fine with me. You're in charge of the tour."

"Then right this way."

She headed toward the athletic courts mostly because they would walk past Mateo and her curiosity was getting the best of her. Apart from Mateo, she was thinking about the conversation, but she'd be damned if she'd ask Josh what it was about.

"So, tell me Isabella. What was it like growing up here?"

Smiling, because honestly there were so many fond memories of living here, she replied, "In one way or another I've lived here my whole life. My father's parents owned this house before my parents. Christmases were magical. My abuela used to decorate the entire house with lights and each room had a separate theme to it. Mostly color themes but when we were all little there were cartoon themed rooms and as we grew those themed rooms changed to more age-appropriate themes. Movies, games, the latest sensation. She was wonderful. Every birthday was special, too. Whatever we wanted for our parties, we always had the best. When she died, my mamá took over, but we were older then and the parties were more sedate but still especially nice. Summers we enjoyed friends, bar-b-ques, music and outdoor parties."

"It sounds like you had a fantastic childhood."

She turned at his wistful tone. "What about you, Josh, what was your childhood like?"

"We didn't have this luxury, but we were loved. My twin, Jax, and my mother, usually argued about something. Most often, Mamá wanted Jax to wear dresses and frilly things and Jax was a diehard tomboy. But, we still had fun. My older brother, Jake, was the best and always made us all laugh. We had parties, lots of family time, especially when my dad was home. His work took him away for periods of time, but when he was home, it was always cause for celebration."

"It sounds like you were raised in love. That's what is most important."

"Yes, we always were loved. Always."

"What does this tomboy sister of yours do now?"

Josh laughed. "She works with me in the security field. She just had twins." He pulled his phone from his back pocket and pulled up his pictures. "Myles and Maya."

Isabella took his offered phone and looked at the pictures of the young twins. Both absolutely gorgeous, both wearing little jeans and white t-shirts. "I see no frilly clothes for Maya."

He laughed. "My mamá is there now helping Jax with the twins and she tries to put Maya in dresses when she can, much to Jax's irritation. But Dodge, my brother-in-law, likes seeing her in girly things. He's the only man who could ever somewhat tame Jax, and that only sparingly. He does manage to persuade her to do or see things his way or someone else's. But in the end, he loves her just the way she is."

They walked along the tennis court, basketball court and kept going. She enjoyed listening to him talk about his family.

"What about your brother Jake, does he also work with you?"

Josh sighed heavily and she turned to see the beautiful smile on his face fall. "Jake died a few years ago. He did work with us, but was..." he cleared his throat. "He was murdered while on the job, same as my father."

She felt bad for bringing it up. She lay her hand on his arm and he stopped walking. "I'm so sorry for your loss."

When his eyes met hers, a sadness had clouded them. "Thank you."

The softness in his tone compelled her to reach up and cup the side of his face. His skin was warm and slightly bristly where he'd shaved but the whiskers were beginning to grow back. He swallowed and leaned forward slowly.

His soft lips touched hers, then pressed firmly against them. He moved his lips slowly and it was as if she were in a trance. Unable to stop or pull away. She could feel his tongue against her lips, asking permission to come in and she wanted to say no. But it was as if he were controlling her every move and her lips parted as his tongue, warm and soft and sexy, tangled with hers in the most delicious kiss she'd ever experienced. Ever.

8

Isabella pulled back, her skin slightly reddened, the pulse in her neck beating wildly and the dazed look in her eyes told him everything he needed to know. She felt it, too.

"I can't..." She swallowed, "I should get back to the wedding."

"Have dinner with me tomorrow night. I'll be back in Texas and I'll meet you wherever you say you'll be."

She took a deep breath. "I can't, Josh."

"Can't? Or don't want to?"

She looked around and he knew she didn't want to say.

"Look, Josh, I just don't see that getting involved is a good idea. We live far apart and a long-distance relationship is not in the works for me."

He smiled but it smarted. "I only asked you to dinner. I don't recall talking about a relationship."

Her cheeks turned a beautiful shade of red. "I didn't mean to make that sound so..."

He chuckled. "I like you, Isabella. You're beautiful,

smart, confident and I haven't met many women like you in my life. And, if you ever tell my mother or Jax I've said that, I'll straight up lie."

She giggled and he loved watching her. She rivaled the sun when she smiled. Bright. Warm. All the things you think of when you think of the sun. His breath caught in his throat.

She took a step back. "It just isn't a good thing right now. I'm sorry."

"Okay. I won't pressure you."

He turned to resume their walk, managed to settle his churning stomach down, and decided to try not to be disappointed about her refusal to have dinner with him. But, if he had the opportunity to see her in the near future, he'd take it for sure. Pulling his phone from his pocket, he asked, "What's your phone number? And before you get all flustered, I just want to text you my number. It's just in case you change your mind or need anything."

"Josh."

"You never know."

She told him her phone number and he sent her a text with his number. "Just in case."

They walked on around the Koi ponds, the gardens and then back to the party. Mateo was off alone, a bit sullen and jittery, drinking and scratching his head and rubbing the back of his neck often.

"Is Mateo having a bad day?"

His movements were so robotic, it was hard not to look away.

Isabella let out a long breath, "He's involved in something again. It seems to be a way of life for him."

"So, this is common?"

She shrugged, "Somewhat. It's the main reason I moved away. And, sadly, my parents are enablers. They constantly fix things for him."

He nodded, but his eyes kept darting over to Mateo.

"There you two are."

He looked up to see Bianca walking toward them, a serene smile on her face.

"Mamá, stop with the matchmaking. I'll make this easy for you. Josh asked me to dinner, and I said no. So, if you've asked him to ask me out, you can now know he did, but I won't."

What? He turned to face Isabella his brows bunched together. "Isabella, your mom didn't ask me to ask you out. Is that what you thought?"

Bianca stepped forward. "Isi, we'd never do such a thing. You are a smart, beautiful, and lovely woman. We are quite certain you can find dates. Why would you think such a thing?"

She looked at her mamá, and Josh wondered what was going through her mind. He could see the differing emotions on her face.

"I saw you take Josh inside and you both emerged later, then you asked me to show him around the grounds. I assumed you were trying to make a match."

She turned to him. "I owe you an apology. I'm very sorry."

Bianca took Isabella's hands in hers. "Isi, Papa wanted to thank Josh and offered to pay for his hotel as our way of saying thank you for taking such good care of Eric. We never asked him to take care of you."

Josh interjected. "I refused, just so you know. A good person doesn't take money for helping another."

Mateo's raised voice caught his attention once again.

Mateo, sitting alone at a small bistro table to the side of the property, sounded agitated. His facial expressions hardened and the force with which he jabbed his finger into the table as he spoke showed anger.

Bianca smiled at him, then pardoned herself. "Excuse me, please."

She gracefully floated down the stairs to the lawn level and over to Mateo's table. The way he looked at her when she approached was almost frightening. He then softened his features, ended his call and turned to face his mother. They chatted softly for a few moments, then Bianca left to speak with some guests, but she was clearly bothered by whatever Mateo had said to her. Her left hand lay against her stomach, as if she were holding something down.

Isabella's brows furrowed and her expression hardened as well. "Now he has Mamá unsettled. This is what happens all the time. You are fortunate to have had upstanding siblings and one remaining such sibling."

"That doesn't mean we always agree."

He watched her graceful shoulders relax and her features soften.

"Of course not. It's just frustrating, that's all." Isabella took a deep breath.

"I should go and visit with relatives, Josh."

"Of course, go on, my friends are right where I left them."

He walked to the table where Diego, Travis and Shep still sat. They were laughing and having a good time and he thought in that moment that things had gotten heavy and laughing with friends seemed like a balm to ease this new wound to his pride.

"She turned you down?" Shep jibbed.

"Yep. She's not interested. Her loss." He tried smiling but he could tell they knew it was forced.

Diego leaned in. "Her brother over there is a rather volatile sort."

He looked at Mateo once again; he was back on his phone.

9

Isabella woke to her mother knocking on her door.

"Isi, may I come in?"

Struggling to sit up, she glanced at her phone on the nightstand to check the time. Eight in the morning. She'd gotten a total of four hours sleep. So not enough.

"Yes, Mamá, come in."

She finger-combed her hair, hoping it wasn't a total loss, but with all the hairspray and other products in it, no doubt it was.

"Good morning, Isi. I'm sorry to come in so early when you haven't slept long at all, but have you seen or heard from Mateo?"

"No, Mamá, I haven't seen him since around midnight. I assumed he came inside and went to bed."

"His bed hasn't been slept in. He's nowhere to be found in the house. When your Papa and I went to bed late last night, he was outside talking to some friends."

"He was acting very strangely yesterday. Eric even commented about it."

Her mother wrung her hands and paced the room.

"I'm afraid he is in trouble again, Isi. I know this irritates you, but his behavior has been off, and he's not been himself for a few days now. Could it be possible that he went back to Texas with Josh and his friends? Do you have Josh's number? If so, would you call and ask, Isi? I want to turn over every stone."

"I do have his number, but, Mamá, if this is your attempt to try and push Josh and me together, please don't."

Her lack of sleep made her crabby and to awaken to one more of Mateo's calamities surely didn't help.

Her mother sat at the edge of her bed and looked into her eyes. The worry she saw in her Mamá's eyes was true.

"Oh no, Isi, I think Josh is wonderful and you are certainly making a mistake to not pursue him, but this is entirely to make sure Mateo didn't go back to Texas with them."

"Why would you think Mateo would go back with them? They barely spoke to him yesterday. Actually, Mateo barely spoke to anyone yesterday. And did you ever find out how he got that black-eye?"

"He refused to talk about it, but I think all the phone calls yesterday had something to do with that."

Isabella took a deep breath and let it out slowly. She should have left sooner. She looked through her texts to find Josh's. "Just in case." It was almost as if he was psychic.

She tapped the phone number he listed in his text and listened as the phone rang. After several rings, she hung up without leaving a voicemail. What could she say? Do you have my brother with you?

"He didn't answer. Let me use the bathroom and I'll try again, Mamá. I'll come and find you. I have to leave early today for work tomorrow so I have to get moving anyway."

"Thank you, Mija."

Her mother stood, her shoulders slightly drooped in defeat, and walked to the door. Isabella vowed if Mateo did this to her parents again, she'd kick him squarely in the nuts so he'd remember how it felt to hurt others.

Taking a deep breath, she went into her bathroom and turned the shower on to heat up. After using the toilet, she stopped at the sink and looked in the mirror. What a fright. She remembered pulling the bobby pins from her hair before she slept last night, but she'd been tired and a little tipsy. After watching Josh get into the coach bus her father secured for their trip, she downed a strong shot of tequila and then instantly regretted it. He looked at her once more before getting on the bus. He'd nodded and smiled and she almost ran to him to ask him to have dinner tonight. But then he was gone.

Emiliana told her she was a fool, but he worked in a dangerous job. His father and brother both died while working in the same job. That wasn't the life for her. The constant worry about whether or not he'd be killed in the line of duty every time he walked out of the house would be too much. Then she worried that she'd never see him again anyway and whether she'd made the biggest mistake of them all in not trying to get to know someone as wonderful as he was, even for a short time?

Shaking her head, she undressed and stepped in the shower, hoping it would revive her for the long day ahead.

Towel drying her hair, she walked out to her bedroom

to find a steaming cup of coffee alongside the bed and a chocolate kiss. Her mamá always made her feel like a little girl in so many ways. Chocolate kisses were her favorite and to have one with her coffee in the morning was a memory she'd always treasure.

Sitting on the side of the bed, she sipped her hot coffee and unwrapped the foil on the kiss. Popping it into her mouth, she savored the creamy chocolate as it mixed with the coffee on her tongue. Today was beginning to look up.

Picking up her phone once again, she dialed the number Josh had sent her and listened as the phone rang a few times without answer. Just as she was about to hang up, his tired voice made her heart flutter.

"Masters."

"Josh?"

She heard rustling noises and the naughty thoughts that went through her mind at that moment made her squeeze her thighs together. He was likely naked.

"Good morning, Isabella. What a nice way to wake up."

Her cheeks flamed red and she was grateful he couldn't see her.

"I'm glad you think so. I actually called to see if Mateo went back to the States with you and your friends."

"Mateo. No. Well, I don't think so. There were a few people on the coach your father commissioned that were in the back, but I'll be honest and say that I plopped in the first available seat and fell asleep. I'm happy to check with my friends and see if they saw him."

"I appreciate it, Josh. He isn't here and he didn't sleep here last night and Mamá is worried sick."

More rustling of linens in the background and her

thoughts went to his body and the definition she'd seen when his wet shirt had clung to him. Handsome, smart, built, he was a catch for some lucky woman, that's a fact.

"Okay. So, let me make a few phone calls and I'll call you back."

10

Running his hands down his face, Josh swiped his eyes to wake himself up. Tossing the covers back, he stepped out of bed and walked across the carpeted floor of the hotel to the bathroom. Using the facilities, he splashed water on his face, brushed his teeth, and then walked back to the bed and retrieved his phone from the nightstand.

He dialed Diego's number; it rang twice before he heard his friend's gravelly voice. "Yeah." "Morning. Did Mateo come back with us on the bus last night? I didn't see him on the bus, but I sat close to the front and zonked out as soon as I was on."

Diego yawned on the other end of the phone. "Naw, I didn't see him on the bus at all."

"Okay. Thanks. I'll check with Travis and Shep."

"Hey, let me know what you find out."

"Sure thing."

He repeated the same call to Travis and got the same response. Then called Shep.

"Naw, I saw him get in a pickup truck around eleven

thirty last night. He seemed reluctant to go but I assumed because it was his brother's wedding and all. We left before he got back though."

"Apparently, he never made it back, Shep. What kind of truck? Color? Anything special about it?"

Shep sighed deeply, coulda been a yawn, but it was something, then his voice cleared slightly as he responded.

"Black pickup, Ford, F-250, light bar on top, chrome rims with knockoffs."

"Wow, you took stock."

"It was a hot truck, Bud. I've been eyeing one myself recently, so it caught my attention."

"Thanks, Shep. I'll relay the information to the Martinez family."

Shep chuckled but said nothing more. Josh ended the call and promptly called Isabella.

"Hi, Josh, any news?"

"Shep said he saw Mateo get into a pickup truck last night around eleven thirty. Black pickup, Ford, F-250, light bar on top, chrome rims with knockoffs. Does this ring a bell with you?"

"I'm not sure. I'll let Papa know."

The hesitation in her voice told him she knew more than she was letting on.

"Isabella, please remember what I do for a living. If I can be of help, please let me."

"Josh, thank you, you've helped a lot."

The line went dead, and he had a sick feeling that something was very wrong indeed. He'd give her some time and try calling again. He couldn't help but wonder why she wouldn't let him help her. It was likely to do with this invisible barrier she'd erected between them for some strange reason. When he had kissed her yesterday, she felt it, too. It was electric. Her face had flushed and her breathing became erratic. They had chemistry. They had something that didn't come along every day and it boggled his mind why. Why didn't she care? But, more importantly, why did he care?

He headed to the bathroom once more and turned on the shower. Standing under the stream of water, he closed his eyes and let it flow over him. That's when he remembered the truck. He'd seen it the night of the bachelor party. He watched from the window of the bar as Mateo had left with the guys in the truck and showed up the next day with a black-eye.

He finished his shower and quickly dressed, grabbed his phone and dialed Isabella. She didn't answer and disappointment ran through him when her voicemail clicked on.

"Isabella, please give me a call. I just remembered something."

He hung up then called Diego.

"Yeah."

"I'm going down to the restaurant to eat something."

"Okay. I'll come with you. I'm up now anyway, someone keeps calling me."

"Fuck off."

Chuckling, Diego ended the call and Josh decided to sit back on the bed and look through some of the pictures he'd taken yesterday. Mostly of Isabella. After a couple of drinks, he'd gotten a little camera happy and started snapping all sorts of pictures. It happened.

He admired how she looked in the sunlight. Her hair so shiny, her skin so clear and beautiful. The light green dress she wore looked gorgeous against her skin. When she smiled, man, she was stunning. No shrinking violet, this woman. She was tough in her own way, practicing medicine every day no doubt made a person tough. She'd taken charge of Eric's inebriation like a pro.

He strapped his gun around his ankle, then he pocketed his phone and wallet and put his watch on.

He heard Diego's door close and strode to his door, pulling it open just before Diego knocked.

"Sorry I woke you up, man."

Diego sighed. "I don't sleep much these days, bro, so no worries."

"PTSD still have its grip on you?"

"Yeah."

Diego pushed the down button on the wall next to the elevator and they both waited in silence as the elevator continued making its stops on the floors below.

The doors opened and both men stepped in.

"You know, my boss's niece was injured in Afghanistan this past year and she's now in a recovery program being retrained for something else. Sponsored by the U.S. military. Let me find out what that entails and see if you qualify."

"Man, I've been through different programs. They usually just tell you to focus on something during an episode or whatever. I'm struggling to work nine to five and the lack of sleep doesn't help. At this point, I'd sell my convenience store and try something else, but it's the only income I have."

The doors opened and they stepped off the elevator and walked down the hall to the restaurant in the hotel.

The sign at the doorway asked them to wait to be seated so they stood looking around. Josh knew he'd call Gaige a bit later and get the information on what Emersyn was doing and what program she was in. She was a go-getter, and he knew Diego would absolutely thrive if he had focus and assistance with his PTSD.

"Just two this morning?" The hostess asked.

Diego responded. "Seat us at a table for four, we may have some friends joining us."

Grateful that Diego had called Travis and Shep, since Josh had been too focused on Isabella to call, he took a deep breath and let out a relieved one. Diego was the care-taker in their bunch. The helper. The man who always ensured everyone was taken care of. It was easy to rely on that.

After he called Gaige, he'd try Isabella again. Maybe this time he'd get more information about what Mateo was up to.

11

Listening to Josh's voicemail Isabella took a deep breath and let it out. He remembered something else. She could feel herself being pulled into Mateo's crap again and it was beginning to piss her off. Time and again this very thing happened. Her parents relied on her to be the responsible one. The one who pulled things together. How many times had she made plans only to have Mateo's latest trouble come first.

She tossed her phone on her bed and continued to pack her clothes into her suitcase. Pulling items from the drawers of her childhood bedroom, she lay them neatly in her bag. She took care with her clothing, her abuela taught her that. Just because they were fortunate to have money to buy expensive things didn't mean they should be irresponsible with what they had. Her brother should have paid closer attention. It irritated her even further because his actions reflected on the whole family. They all looked like spoiled, wayward brats when one of them behaved like one.

"There you are." She turned at her mother's voice.

"Hi, Mamá. I wanted to get my packing finished this morning."

"Yes. Will you come down and have breakfast with us before guests arrive for the gift opening?"

"I don't think I can stay for the gift opening, Mamá. I've got to get going. I'll be driving for a few hours today."

"Oh, Isi. I miss you so much and wish your visits home weren't so short."

She turned and looked into her mother's sad eyes. "I know, Mamá. Why don't you plan to come and stay with me in Texas for a week? We'll do girl things like pedicures, shopping, having our hair done and maybe facials. We'll stay up late and watch movies and talk."

"Oh, Isi, that sounds just wonderful."

Her mother's arms wrapped around her and she eagerly hugged her back, hoping the trip to Texas would happen soon. She held tightly and tried to pour her love and affection into her hug.

"I'll expect you to visit now."

"Maybe once we find Mateo and make sure he's all right, I'll give you a call and we'll make plans."

Her body deflated at her mother's words. There it was again.

Pulling away from her, her mother held onto her shoulders and looked deeply into her eyes.

"I know you and your brother have differences, Isi. He's never been as strong or as smart as you. In some ways he is so jealous of the ease with which you seem to float through life and succeed at everything you do."

"I don't float through life. That's what no one understands, Mamá. When I was in med school, I was in the library working until one or two in the morning while Mateo and Emiliana and Eric were partying with friends and having fun. I was interning in the wee hours of the morning while they were at dances and get-togethers and having parties. I was working sixteen-hour days when they started working for Papa, maybe putting in six hours a day. That's what no one wants to see. It's easy to wave their hands and say, 'everything comes easy for Isi', because they don't look at the work."

"Sweetheart, we know. We've seen it. We do understand. But none of your siblings would ever be able to devote the time and energy to one thing like you did. That's the difference. You are special in that respect."

She closed her eyes. This argument had taken place repeatedly and it was the equivalent of talking to the stone walls outside.

She pulled away and turned to her dresser, pulled out her makeup and tucked it in the zippered bag she'd used to bring it here. Her mother stood in the room silent and Isabella knew if she looked at her, she'd cave in. Deciding instead to continue packing, she remained silent. She tucked her makeup into a side zipper pouch and turned to the closet once more. Her mother stood in her path. "Just come and have breakfast, Isi."

Swallowing the feeling that she was hurting her mother, she sighed. "All right."

Her mother turned toward the door, a soft smile adorning her face. Isabella took a deep breath as she opened the door for her mother, whose silent persistence made it impossible to resist her will. It rather pissed Isi off that she was caving once again. She'd always be the good daughter.

Her mother locked her arm in Isabella's as they made their way silently down the stairs to the lower level. The sun shone brightly through the windows of the great room, lighting everything in a different color today than it had been last night. It was one of the things she so loved about this house. In the light of day, the stone on the walls looked varying shades of yellows, oranges and golds. In the evening, without the sun's rays on them, the stone walls were grays and tans and browns. The same room took on different personalities depending on the time of day. It was mesmerizing.

The staircase curved onto the first floor. The gorgeous dark oak rails and finishes on the staircase and the built-in bookcases added a depth and beauty to the overall look in this room. Her mother's touches of orange, gold and yellow pillows on the sofa and chairs added the pops of colors that brightened the dark wooden fixtures. They created a comfortable area to sit and chat, have a drink or simply to admire as you walked down the grand staircase to the main level.

The aroma of bacon and coffee summoned her senses and she was suddenly hungry. Prior to smelling breakfast, she hadn't felt hungry at all. She'd been focusing on her anger instead.

Her father's phone rang as they walked into the dining room.

He answered and immediately said, "Oh, no. Where?"

12

After Josh and Diego ordered their breakfasts, Josh texted Gaige to ask about his niece.

Josh broke the silence. "So, if you sell your convenience store, what would you do?"

"I don't know. I guess when I was in the Army I wanted to be out. But, now that I'm out and feel damaged, it seems like I should have stayed in. Civi life doesn't seem to work for me. I never know when these attacks will come on—a weird sound, a strange movement from a stranger, the television, the radio, or a car horn—it's random. So I have trouble sleeping, which means doing the daytime work is a struggle. And, frankly, I just don't feel like I'm doing anything meaningful."

Diego drank down some of his coffee, added sugar and stirred it. His hands shook slightly, which could be from the lack of sleep. Unfortunately, he wouldn't be able to work at GHOST because of the severity of his PTSD. He could hear something, gunfire or some other activity (or disruption) that could trigger an episode on a mission. Diego needed some intense therapy and maybe occupational retraining. Something he found worthwhile. And a dog. A therapy dog. He should have stayed in closer contact with Diego.

"I get that."

Josh's phone chimed and he grabbed it from the table. Seeing a message from Gaige, he tamped down his disappointment.

"Listen, Diego, keep an open mind on this, okay?" He read the message fully then said, "So my boss, Gaige's, niece Emersyn was injured when her convoy was hit with IEDs in Afghanistan. She was thrown from her MRAP and tossed several feet away, landing on rock and vehicle parts. Her hip was damaged severely, along with other injuries, but she's recovering. She won't be able to go back into the field due to limited mobility, but the U.S. Government is secretly bringing injured veterans into a training program, Operation Live Again. The retraining is to help disabled and injured veterans learn how to find, track and apprehend, through special ops and in concert with local PDs and the military, child pornographers, traffickers and kidnappers. She's been accepted into the program. They have openings. You should try to get in, Diego."

Diego listened, and Josh watched his face as the information was processed. "What if I couldn't do it?"

"What if you could?"

Diego fidgeted in his seat and picked at his breakfast.

"Look, no pressure. But, I'll text you the information on how to apply to the program and then you can give it some thought. You said meaningful. What could be more meaningful than saving kids?"

"I might fail and that would be worse."

"And, you probably will succeed. Just think about that."

Diego nodded and Josh saw his eyes well with moisture. He was certainly in need of something like this. For a fact.

"There they are. You made me hungry, bro." Shep jibbed at Diego.

Diego's response was more lighthearted than he actually was. "Sorry, but the breakfast is good."

Shep and Travis sat at the table and the waitress brought them coffee.

Travis looked across the table to Josh. "Did they find Mateo yet?"

"I haven't heard. I'm waiting to hear back from Isabella."

Shep chuckled and Josh just shook his head.

Travis then picked up the conversation. "So today, we have to have our tuxes fitted; Sofia has been bugging me. So can we get this done before we do anything else?"

Josh chuckled. "We'll put you out of your misery."

The rest of them laughed, and so did Travis, for which he was grateful. Finishing up breakfast, Josh looked at his phone again; still no word from Isabella. As they walked out to Travis' car, he dialed her number again. As he listened to her phone ring his gut tightened, and he wondered what was going on that she suddenly clammed up and didn't want to talk to him. He thought about leaving the information about the truck on her voicemail but then decided against it. Part of him wanted to talk to her again. To hear her voice. Part of him, his GHOST part, wanted to know what the hell was going on. That part of him was beginning to get more curious and concerned as time moved on.

He simply said, "Isabella, call me. I've remembered something you should know."

Climbing in the passenger seat after Shep and Diego took the backseat, Josh sat back and tried to relax but he was beginning to think that he wouldn't be relaxing today.

"After we get fitted, what should we do today? Anyone up for a game of golf?" Travis asked.

Josh laughed. "Man, I've never golfed."

Diego added, "Me neither and no I don't want to learn."

Shep and Travis wanted to golf, and Josh thought maybe he and Diego would go on a road trip to the Martinez's house and see what they could do to help. It might help Diego also.

Travis pulled into the tuxedo rental shop and they all got out of the car. Josh walked in alongside Diego. "I'm going out to the Martinez's house to see if I can help them piece together Mateo's last steps. How about you come with me and let these guys get their golf game in."

"That sounds like a lot more fun than golf."

"We'll see how fun it is, but it will likely be more useful than hacking at the ground all day with a stick."

"That's for damned sure."

"Plus, we'll get a bit of a road trip in and maybe eat some great Mexican food for lunch."

"Deal." Diego cleared his throat. "I haven't had good honest to goodness Mexican food in a longtime. Now I'm hungry again."

Josh chuckled. And he'd see Isabella again.

13

Her father's business emergency was a usual happening in their household. Her brothers had taken over parts of the business to alleviate some of this burden as her father aged, but with Mateo's disappearance, and Eric on his honeymoon, someone had to pick up the slack and that job fell to her father. If Mateo didn't become more responsible, he would find himself out of a job and someone else would be taking his place.

Bianca hugged her husband and reminded him that guests would be here beginning in an hour to open the wedding gifts.

"I know, querida, I'll come back as soon as I can." He waved to Emiliana and Isabella before stepping out of the room.

Wringing her hands, Bianca sat at the table with her daughters and wrapped her hands around her coffee cup and sighed deeply.

"Mamá, it will be all right. Emi and I will be here with

you. Eric and Cecily will be home soon, too. And Mateo will come dragging in expecting that no one will be angry with him, as he always does, without thought to his disrespect."

"Isi, not now."

Isabella looked over at Emi and received a shrug in return.

Eric and Cecily entered the dining room just as Isabella finished her breakfast.

"Good morning, everyone." Her brother beamed. Clearly Cecily had forgiven him. And he'd had some sleep last night, so he was happy and refreshed.

Her mother feigned a smile, "Good morning, Eric and Cecily. Will you join us for breakfast?"

Cecily smiled. Her light brown hair was the perfect complement to her eyes which were a light caramel. She smiled from ear to ear this morning and the new ring on her finger glittered in the sun that streamed in through the large dining room windows.

Eric pulled a chair out for Cecily, then leaned down and kissed the top of her head before sitting himself. Watching them made Isabella happy. While she never worried yesterday that the wedding would be called off, she did worry that it would have been more tense and uncomfortable with Eric and Ceci fighting. In the end, once Ceci had her wedding dress on, and the guests began arriving, she focused more on the wedding and the day than the fact that Eric had behaved poorly the night before. Boys having fun and all, and his friends had all at one time or another at the reception told Ceci they were sorry for encouraging him to drink so much. That had seemed to lighten her anger somewhat.

Eric looked at the head of the table where their father usually sat.

"Where's Papa?"

Emiliana shook her head. "Work issue. Mateo didn't come home last night and someone had to deal with it. He said he'd be home as soon as he could."

"Where's Mateo? Does anyone know? He wouldn't tell me what happened to his eye yesterday, but does anyone have a clue?"

Isabella shook her head. "He's been quiet about whatever happened. I saw him on the phone a lot yesterday and he remained off by himself most of the day. His behavior is very strange these days."

Elisa brought plates and coffees out for both Eric and Ceci and they went to the sideboard to fill them with breakfast goodies.

Weekends were relaxed like this here. She did miss this part of being home. Elisa took extraordinary care of their family and had for many years. The Martinez family paid her well, gave her benefits and insurance and she'd been happy to work for them. When Elisa's children were younger, they worked at the Estate for summer money and they used to beam from ear to ear on payday. Mr. Martinez had also set up college funds for Elisa's children, telling them if they contributed ten percent of their wages to the fund, so would he. It was his way of helping out but also teaching them a good work ethic and Elisa had thanked her parents frequently for the generous contributions for them. In the end, both of her children had been able to afford college and they were both successful in their chosen fields.

Isabella looked at Ceci as she sat to eat her breakfast.

"So, after the gift opening, where are you going on your honeymoon?"

Ceci beamed. "Eric surprised me with a three-week trip to Europe. We'll be touring castles and hiking and eating in fantastic restaurants."

Emiliana clapped her hands together. "Very nice, brother, very nice."

Eric smiled. "We have tickets for a couple of shows. We'll be seeing the Louvre in Paris. Then we're off to London and then Scotland."

"You will be exhausted when you return." Bianca smiled. "Your father and I went to Europe for our twentieth anniversary. It was magical."

The doorbell rang and Bianca glanced at the clock on the sideboard, then stood to answer it. "I wonder if we have early guests."

She left the room and when she opened the door Isabella heard her say, "Josh, Diego, how nice to see you here today."

"Thank you, Mrs. Martinez. I'd like to speak with Isabella if she is available."

"Of course. Have you eaten breakfast?"

"Yes, ma'am. At the hotel."

"Please come in."

Laying her napkin alongside her plate and trying to keep her features neutral, Isabella waited until they appeared in the door to look up. Her face instantly heated and her skin grew warm. He was so incredibly handsome and this morning he looked rested and ready for anything. He was a proud, imposing presence as he stood in the doorway. He was easily a head taller than her mother, broad, lean and strong. He wore jeans, which fit him perfectly, and a black three-button-placket shirt tucked in at the waist.

"Isabella, I left you several messages, but you didn't answer. I remembered something about Mateo and that truck, and I thought we could figure out what may have happened to him.

14

He watched Isabella swallow; her cheeks were tinted a sweet shade of pink which looked lovely on her. Her hair was down today, dark, shiny and falling over her shoulders. Then she licked her lips, and it felt as if things went into slow motion.

"I'm sorry. Yes, I did get a message from you, and I meant to respond, but we came down for breakfast and…"

She looked around for her phone. Her pockets were empty, and when she glanced at the table, her brows furrowed.

"I must have left my phone upstairs."

He slowly let out a breath, she wasn't completely ignoring him.

Bianca motioned to the empty chairs at the table. "Please sit and have some coffee or juice with us."

Diego moved ahead of him and sat at the table next to Eric. They shook hands.

"Congratulations, again."

Eric beamed, "Thank you. Cecily, this is Diego, I'm not sure I introduced you yesterday."

Cecily smiled at Diego as Josh took a seat at the table.

Isabella sat to his left and as Elisa set a cup of coffee in front of Diego and him, she asked, "What did you remember about Mateo and the truck, Josh?"

He glanced at her then at Bianca. "I saw that truck while we were in Texas at the bar. That's where Mateo left us. The truck pulled up alongside the patio we were sitting on and Mateo walked out to it. He talked with someone on the passenger side of the truck and then got in. That was the last we saw of him."

Glancing at Bianca, he continued, "He showed up with a black-eye at the wedding. The same truck picked him up here later last night. And as you know," he glanced once again at Bianca, concerned this was hard for her to hear. The look on her face clearly showed worry about her son. "He was off by himself most of the day yesterday and on a plethora of phone calls. I think it's fair to say something is wrong. If it were related to the Martinez's businesses, he'd speak to your husband and not take off in this truck and certainly not receive a black-eye for it."

Eric leaned forward and caught his eye. "You're correct there, Josh. Our businesses are all legitimate. That is Papa's number one rule."

Josh nodded; Ivan had told him as much when they were in his office yesterday.

Bianca set her coffee cup on the table. "What do you think it means and should we call the authorities?"

Josh shook his head. "Unless you have proof of wrong-doing, the authorities won't be able to help you. They will tell you that guys get into fights all the time and appearances can be deceiving. But, I may be able to. I work for a security firm. We have connections, we have equipment, and part of what we do for a living is find people and ferret out reasons."

Isabella's voice was stern when she said, "So you want us to hire you? You're looking for a job."

"No, I didn't say that. This is personal for me; I've not called anyone at the office yet. But, I've gotten to know you." He nodded to Eric then encompassed all of them with a wave of his hand. "All of you and..." He halted and swallowed. "I feel compelled to help because I know I can. There's something wrong here. I've seen this sort of thing countless times. Mateo's movements, his behavior, leaving and not telling anyone, being secretive, not explaining his black-eye, and now his disappearance all signal something is not right."

Bianca sighed heavily. "I agree with you, Josh. I can feel it in my bones. His behavior the past few days has been very different. What do you need from us to look into this further?"

Josh opened his mouth to speak, but Bianca continued, "And we can pay you for this."

Holding up his hand he said, "Right now, I'm not asking for payment. Until we know there is actually something illegal or nefarious going on, I'd just like to investigate a bit. And," he nodded to Diego, "our buddies wanted to golf today, and we aren't golfers, so you're getting us out of a boring day. I'm here for the week until Travis gets married on Saturday so I have the time. Also, I'm not the type to sit by a pool or lay around; I need something to do and I think you need a hand."

Eric asked, "What do you need then?"

"I need to get into Mateo's house. There may be clues as to what is going on. And perhaps he's there, sleeping off a bad day of drinking at the wedding yesterday and last night. Who knows? But, it seems the first place to start."

Isabella let out a long breath. "I can take you over there." Nodding to her brother she added, "Eric and Cecily have guests coming for their gift opening then they are leaving on their honeymoon. Mamá and Emi need to be here as the hostesses and Papa had to go to the office to take care of something Mateo should be here handling."

"Thank you. I appreciate it."

Bianca smiled at him, her eyes glistened with moisture and her shoulders relaxed slightly. "Thank you, Josh. God sent you from heaven at just the right time for our family."

He shook his head. "I don't know about that Mrs. Martinez..."

"Bianca."

Nodding, "Bianca. If I can do something, I will."

Isabella stood. "I'll finish my packing and then we can go. Please finish your coffees."

He watched her as she walked out of the room. Her posture was straight and proud. Her supple steps, so similar to Bianca's, made her look as if she were gliding out of the room. Once again, he thought of her as if she was too good to be true.

15

Walking to the bathroom to pack up her brush, comb and curling iron, Isabella took another look around to make sure she didn't miss anything. She left her shampoo and conditioner for the next time she'd be home. If she were a betting woman, she'd wager there would be a baby shower in the coming year. Cecily had talked about a houseful of children for a long time.

Isabella stowed her things, closed the top and zipped up her bag. Pulling it off the bed, she lifted the retractable handle and rolled the suitcase to her door. She picked up her medical bag on her way out. From the top of the stairs, she could hear the laughter from the dining room and wondered what they were laughing about. Her emotions were conflicted. First, Eric and Cecily deserved to be light-hearted and jovial. They'd gotten married yesterday so of course their spirits were high. But Mateo was missing and likely in trouble again. That may be no laughing matter. But, she reminded herself, they'd been through so many of Mateo's crises that it was just more for their family.

Isabella held onto the banister as she carried her luggage downstairs. She parked her suitcase next to the front door and headed to the dining room. When she entered the room, Josh and Diego stood and she had to smile. Gallantry was almost nonexistent these days. It was nice to see it.

Her mother stood and walked to her. "Mija, you are radiant as always. Will you be coming back to the house after you take Josh and Diego to Mateo's?"

"No, Mamá, I really have to start driving back. I have to be at work early in the morning."

She turned to Cecily and Eric. They each stood as she approached them. Wrapping Cecily in a warm embrace she whispered to her new sister, "I love you, Ceci. Have the best time on your honeymoon."

"I will, Isi, and don't be afraid to give Josh a chance. The way he looks at you is amazing."

Isabella stood back, her hands on Ceci's shoulders and looked into her sister-in-law's eyes. Ceci smiled and winked and Isabella's cheeks heated.

Moving to Eric, she hugged her brother. "Congratulations, hermano. I love you."

"I love you, too, hermana. Keep me informed of all that transpires. I know Mamá and Papa won't because they won't want me to worry, but I will anyway, so I'd like to know what's happening."

"I will, Eric. Safe travels and have the best honeymoon!"

Walking around the table to Emiliana, she hugged her sister tightly and choked-up. She and Emi were close, and it was always so hard to say goodbye to her. Emi said it for them both.

"I love you, hermana. You share my heart. We are as if we were one. Be careful."

Standing back, she inhaled deeply and let it out slowly. Goodbyes sucked.

Looking at Josh, she tried to summon a smile, which she doubted actually looked like one, but the attempt was there.

"Shall we go then?"

"Yes." He shook Eric's hand. "Have a great honeymoon!"

"Thank you, Josh." Eric replied.

Josh and Diego pushed in their chairs and walked to the front of the house along with Isabella and Bianca.

At the door, Bianca asked, "Josh, will you please let me know what you find and what your thoughts are on this? I can fill my husband in when he returns, and it will ease our minds to know someone is trying to help us."

"Of course, I'll get your number from Isabella at the house."

"Yes. Please."

"And thank you for the coffee."

"You are most welcome."

Her mother kissed her on the cheek then wrapped her in a hug. As she reached for her suitcase, her hand clashed with Josh's.

"I've got this, Isabella."

Her heart fluttered. Her name sounded wonderful and so feminine the way it floated off his tongue and she doubted she'd ever tire of hearing it.

"Thank you. I can carry my medical bag," she quietly responded and walked down the steps to the driveway.

Diego followed them out the door and Josh tossed Diego the keys to his rental. "Follow us, Diego."

Diego's smile crossed his entire face. "Of course."

Butterflies took flight in her tummy, but she kept walking to her car. Pressing the button on her fob, she opened the trunk and watched Josh's muscles form and stretch in his dark shirt as he easily lifted her suitcase and lay it in the trunk. He closed the lid and turned to face her.

"I'm happy to drive, Isabella."

She shook her head no, but then handed the keys over to him. She wasn't thinking clearly. Repeatedly asking herself who this giddy girl inside of her was, she quickly tossed her head and walked to the passenger side of the car. Josh reached forward to open her door and she jumped at his nearness. His scent surrounded her, and she felt lightheaded as it settled all around her. Riding in a car together was going to be bittersweet.

Without looking into his eyes, which was hard, she carefully entered the car, sat and lifted her legs inside. He closed the door and walked around the front of her car and she busied herself with buckling her seatbelt, so she didn't humiliate herself by drooling. But, oh, he was magnificent.

He opened the door and managed to get inside, which for a man his size amazed her. He was around six feet tall, which was probably slightly above average, but compared to her 5'2" was very tall. Yet instead of being clumsy and awkward in his movements, his were sleek and like those of a cat.

He handed her the keys with a smirk, pushed the button on the dash to start the car, then fastened his seatbelt.

"Funny. You didn't mention I wouldn't need the keys to start the car."

"Ooops" She smiled.

"Which direction are we heading?"

"Mateo lives downtown in a loft." She pulled out her phone and searched for Mateo's address.

Entering it into her GPS she noticed the puzzled look on Josh's face.

"I've never been to Mateo's, but I have wondered about it. No one in the family has been there. He's kept it very private for a couple of years now."

Josh's brows bunched together but he said nothing.

"I bet you've been to your sister's house dozens of times."

"Yes, and now with Maya and Myles, I'm there as often as I can be; they're getting so fun to be around."

The directions led them away from the picturesque countryside of La Quemada, where the Martinez's family estate was, to the seedy downtown area of Nuevo Laredo, where Mateo's condo was. The scenery changed from beautiful rolling hills to a smoggy, overly congested city. Whoever would prefer to live here over La Quemada didn't appreciate the beauty of the country or, more likely, had serious problems.

Isabella looked around as if interested in the area. He glanced over at her then back at the road as the traffic increased.

"I've never been to this part of the city before. I don't understand," she absently said.

"Me, either. No surprise."

His attempt at lighthearted conversation ended there. Preoccupied, she quickly looked at the GPS then back at the road and shook her head. "According to the GPS, he lives just four miles from here. This is awful."

He nodded, not sure what to say except that he agreed.

"Where do you live in Texas?"

She looked at him briefly. "I live in Magnolia, which is just outside of Galveston."

"I gather it's nothing like this."

A poor family, not living there by choice, was on the street corner selling vegetables from a cart and she frowned. Though on her it wasn't at all unattractive.

"No. Nothing. Magnolia is a beautiful small town with a big heart. The streets are clean, the businesses are all kept up, even in the downtown area, and the air is clean. It's not congested like this at all. I simply don't understand why Mateo would live in an area like this."

"Hopefully we'll find some answers at his place."

The GPS told them to turn left onto Center Street which looked very much like the last street they were on. The buildings were older, some of them not well managed. Garbage cans lined the street on either side, some of them overflowing. The smell had taken an odd turn, the air now stale and sometimes ripe. The GPS spoke once more and told them to turn right onto Revolution and suddenly the area improved somewhat. The air still had a yellow cast to it. The cars parked in the street were a landing place for the light-colored dust dulling their shine.

Up ahead was a large building. The brightly colored stone on the outside looked fairly new as it still hadn't been discolored from the condition of the air.

"That's it." Isabella pointed to the colorful building.

"Do you have keys?"

"My mother sent me the passcode for entry."

"No one in your family has been here but she has the passcode?"

She glanced at him. "She insisted on it in case of an

emergency. She has the passcodes or keys to all of our places."

He nodded. "Makes sense."

Isabella pointed to a sign. "There is a parking garage down below."

He turned into the lower parking area and noticed they were all numbered. "Which one should I park in?"

Looking at her phone, she read the address. "Numbers 23 and 24 are Mateo's."

Slowly driving past the cars in the garage, he noted that most of the vehicles were newer and parking inside the garage kept the yellow sludge off of the cars. That was a bonus.

He spotted the numbers up ahead. "Number 23 is taken. 24 is open though."

Isabella looked at the car in space 23. "That's Mateo's car."

"How did he drive out to your parents' house for the wedding yesterday?"

She tucked her hair behind her ear and the concern on her face grew. "I don't know. We were all so busy and I was taking care of Eric mostly."

"Yeah. Does Mateo have more than one vehicle?"

"Not that I know of."

Josh watched in the mirror as Diego found an empty spot that said visitor. He took a deep breath. They just might be walking into something she'd probably not want to see. His gut told him this was bad. His brain told him the same thing.

"Isi, do you want to stay here? Maybe you don't want to see...if things are bad, you won't want to see..."

"I'm a doctor, Josh. I've seen more bad things than you have in your security work."

She was totally off-base about that one, but he didn't say so.

"But not a family member."

"If he's in a bad way, I'm the one who can help him."

Josh swallowed and stared into her eyes. He could see the stubbornness there and knew he'd probably not change her mind.

"Okay." He opened his door, unlatched his seatbelt and was out of the car at the same time as Isabella. He'd rather hoped she'd have stayed and let him be a gentleman, but he'd temper his disappointment. For now.

She saw him looking at her medical bag. "Just in case I need it."

They walked to the end of the garage where there was an elevator. The odor was slightly less disgusting here, but the heat made it impossible not to smell the rotting garbage probably a street over. Plus, whatever that yellow haze was in the air smelled like rotting carcasses.

He pushed the up button on the elevator and the doors instantly opened, which he was happy about. He held the doors as Isabella stepped in, then he stepped in and waited for Diego to join them. An air freshener was in the elevator. He assumed the owners of the condos in this building complained to the Condo Board to do something to get rid of the stench from outside. Then why buy here?

"Fucking stinks out there." Diego snapped.

Isabella pushed the button for the top floor and Josh immediately thought that Mateo was living in luxury if he was on the penthouse, if you could call it that. Those units usually went for quite a large sum.

She replied, "It does. It's the rendering plant here in town. They butcher the animals, then burn the fats down and sell them for use in other industries."

The elevator was smooth and fast and there was little time to say anything on the ride up. When the doors opened, they stepped into an alcove and the only door was presumably Mateo's. There was a keypad outside his door and Isabella punched in the number and the door unlocked. She gently pushed it open, but Josh put his hand on her shoulder and tilted his head toward the right, asking her silently to step back. Her brows furrowed slightly, and she opened her mouth, but he held his fingers over his lips, asking for her silence.

Her eyes rounded and she silently stepped back as Josh and Diego stepped forward. Walking cautiously into the large living room area of the penthouse, Josh saw the place was neat and tidy. Nothing out of place and the ultra-modern furniture was such a contrast from his mother's home. The tables were polished iron wood which was very expensive because it was so hard to carve. The shine on them boasted an expensive finish. The glass objects that were placed around the home glittered in the sunlight.

"Mateo?" He called out but heard nothing.

The far wall in the living room had a fireplace with glass marble tiles at the bottom that ran the length of the wall; it was about two feet up from the floor, long and narrow, and very expensive.

He slowly made his way into the room, saw a kitchen to the right and stepped toward it. A dirty glass sat on the counter, but no other dirty dishes were in sight.

"Mateo?" He called once again, turning to see Isabella had followed him into the penthouse. Her brows pulled together tightly as she surveyed the home. Clearly, she was as confused as he was at this point. Josh continued walking through the kitchen, a large area with the most modern stainless appliances, all high grade and of commercial quality.

He stepped through the kitchen to a short hallway with two doors. He stood to the side and opened the first door to see a palatial office with a dark mahogany desk facing the door and a full wall of dark mahogany bookcases behind the desk. Glass and gold mementos or decorations were on the shelves in various places as were some books. A closed laptop lay on the desk. The tall, black-leather chair was pushed in as if the owner always put things right before leaving.

He turned, walked out, and crossed the hall and opened the second door. The bedroom. Overly large and opulent in its décor, it had a huge bed in the center of the far wall. The curtains were of high quality as was the bedspread. There was a floating headboard of chrome and glass and two floating nightstands, one on each side, graced the bed. The bed was made, no clothing or shoes lay around. It was almost as if no one lived here.

Josh crossed the room to the wall of closet doors and opened them up. A neat row of suits was the first thing he saw, and his mind went to Mateo the night of the bachelor party. He wore light khakis with a light-yellow dress shirt tucked in. No tie, no suit. Which he wouldn't wear. But even yesterday, at the wedding of his brother in which he was the best man, Mateo instantly took off his jacket and loosened his tie after the ceremony. That didn't give the impression of someone as buttoned-up and staunch as this place was.

Isabella walked into the room and the look on her face said it all.

This was unbelievable. How could Mateo afford all of this? They had wealth, certainly. But not like this. Not this extravagant. The furniture was expensive. Very expensive. She walked to the bed and lifted the comforter to read the maker on the frame of the bed.

"Fendi Casa."

Diego stepped into the room. "There's another bedroom down the hall. Neat as a pin."

She continued to check the manufacturer on the pieces of furniture and found them all to be Fendi Casa. "I'm sure my father pays Mateo well for his work at the Martinez Water Division, but not this well. There's no way. This is very expensive furniture. And even if he could afford a couple of pieces of it, all of this is Fendi Casa. It's unbelievable."

She pulled her phone from her pocket and began to scroll through her contacts. She stopped then. Who should she call? Her father? Eric? Her mother? Emi?

"I don't know who would know Mateo better or who to call. He's always been off doing his own thing and the rest of us just lived our lives without him."

Josh looked at her. "I would start with your father. Find out what Mateo is making for a salary. Maybe he got bonuses for performance and bought this furniture from that."

"Still, this place..." She turned and looked around. "This isn't Mateo. I'm dumbfounded at this opulence. This..."

Confusion showed on her face. He felt sorry for her.

"I'm a little afraid to be honest. I don't know if I'll be enraged if I find that Papa was paying him like this while I've been working day and night to earn a living helping people or if I'll be enraged that he didn't and Mateo is doing something illegal to earn this wealth."

Diego spoke from the back of the room. "Sounds like you'll be pissed either way."

She turned and looked at Diego and he shrugged.

In the end she dialed her father and listened as the phone rang without answer. Finally receiving his voice-mail, she left a message. "Papa, it's Isi. Please call me when you get this message. It's important and about Mateo."

She immediately found her mother's picture in her phone and tapped it. Putting the phone to her ear she listened to the ringing on the other end.

"Isi, what have you found out?"

"Mamá, do you have any idea how much money Mateo makes working for Papa?"

Her mother hesitated for just a second or two. "I believe Mateo and Eric each make the same salary. A little more than two million pesos each year. Around $100,000 American dollars."

Isabella sat hard on the edge of Mateo's bed.

"Why do you need to know this, Isi?"

"Mamá, did you know Mateo's home is filled with Fendi Casa furniture and glass sculptures and top of the line appliances and he has Italian-made suits in his closet?"

"Oh, I don't see how he could afford..." Her mother stopped talking and dread filled her stomach instantly.

"I tried calling Papa but he didn't answer. Is he home yet?"

"No, he hasn't made it home. I tried calling a while ago, too. He's been gone much longer than he should have been. The emergency he spoke of this morning was only that a shipment had been delayed and the workers needed direction as to how to fulfill the orders for today without it. Nothing that should have taken so long."

She felt as though she'd throw-up. A phone ringing from the other room had them all turning their heads toward the sound.

"Mamá, I have to go."

Josh and Diego both stepped out of the bedroom and she listened not sure she wanted to know what was going on.

But she followed them anyway to the office where they both stood, the top drawer of the desk opened, and they stared at the phone. Josh pulled the phone from the drawer and gently lay it on top of the desk. He then pulled his own cell phone out and dialed a number.

Mateo's phone stopped ringing.

"Gaige, this is Josh. Say, can you send a signal through my phone to check and see if a phone is bugged? Or, if it's set to detonate something?"

Her stomach flopped as she listened to his end of the conversation.

"Okay, do it now."

Josh then pulled his phone from his ear and put it on speaker. He then held his phone just above Mateo's phone and looked at her and Diego and held his finger over his lips. A slight beeping sound came from his phone and Mateo's phone began to ring again.

Josh looked at the readout on the phone and she and Diego stepped closer to read the name of the caller.

"Unknown."

Then the voice of whoever Josh was speaking to said, "All clear."

"Thanks, Gaige. I just may need some assistance here. Is someone available should I need it?"

Mateo's phone then stopped ringing.

"Yeah, we've got a couple operatives available. Falcon is now onboard, and Hawk is here."

"Thanks, I'll call you later to let you know and fill you in."

"Roger."

The call ended and Isabella watched him pick up Mateo's phone. Just then it began ringing again.

This time Josh answered it on speaker.

"Hello."

A vacant sounding voice responded. "I see you're finally interested in talking to me. We're watching Mateo's penthouse. I know you're in there. You need to listen carefully. We have Mateo and we won't let him go until we get what's ours. My shipment of guns is missing, and Mateo keeps telling me he doesn't know anything about guns, but I think he does. So, if I don't have my guns in one day,

I'll begin cutting off Mateo's fingers, one at a time and leaving them right there on the top of the desk for you to find. And, if you think for one minute that having the place watched to catch me is wise, Isabella will be next."

The line went dead, and Josh turned to look at her.

18

Guns. Mateo somehow got himself involved in gun trafficking.

"Isi, think hard on this. How would Mateo be involved in transporting guns? Can you think of any friends or acquaintances of Mateo's that would be involved in this?"

Isabella sat hard in a chair across from the desk.

Josh looked at Diego. "You okay?"

"Yeah."

Pulling his phone up, Josh dialed Gaige.

"Vickers."

"I need help. I think we're involved in gun trafficking, likely over the U.S./Mexico border. Plus, kidnapping. Isabella Martinez's brother, Mateo, is being held hostage at the moment and Isabella's life has just been threatened."

"Okay. We getting payment on this one?"

"Not sure. It's kind of personal. But, being that illegal export of guns is involved, you want to contact Casper and see if payment will come from above his paygrade?"

"Yep. I'll keep in touch. You can expect Hawk and Falcon as soon as we can get the plane ready and flight plan filed."

"Roger. Thank you."

"Out."

The line went dead, and he looked at Isabella then Diego.

"We have help coming from two of my coworkers. That doesn't mean it'll be easy, but it will be easier with trained professionals."

He walked to Isabella and squatted down in front of her. Taking her hands in his, he felt the chill and saw the fear in her eyes.

"As for you, you can't go home. You don't have protection and you don't know where, when or how they'll be coming. We have to trust that he means it when he says he's watching."

Her head shook. "Where will I go? I don't want to go to my parents. It'll bring them there."

He inhaled deeply then said, "When Hawk and Falcon get to Texas, we'll find a house to rent, an Airbnb or something we can secure. It's what we do. Failing that, we'll come up with something else. But we'll need a place to set up operations, computers, etc. It'll keep them off us for a while as we search for Mateo and set up the ops."

"But, I have work..."

"Not until you're safe. Not until this is over."

"Josh, my practice. My patients will need me to..."

"If you are kidnapped, or killed, your practice will mean nothing, and your patients won't have you anyway. And, what if you go back and they follow you and one of your patients or coworkers is caught up in this mess and injured or worse? I know you don't want that."

Her shoulders sank and he felt sorry for her.

"Diego, are you okay to drive when we leave here?"

"Yes. I want in."

"Diego..."

"I want in. I feel alive right now. I feel useful. Meaningful."

"But you're PTSD could be a hinderance."

Diego scratched his forehead lightly with his thumbnail. "Look, I'll stay out of the way and only do as asked. You wanted me to think about this, I'm thinking about it."

"But this is different than what Emmy is doing."

"I get it, but it's a start to see if this will work. I'll have a better idea of what I'm up against if I know whether this type of on-the-edge work is for me. And, if it's too much, I'll know my limitations. No way will I get in the way to get Isabella or anyone else hurt."

Josh looked over at Isabella. She watched them with interest and saw the doctor in her snap to attention when Diego talked about his PTSD. Maybe they'd be able to help each other keep their minds off of the bad shit they could be getting involved in if he kept them both close.

Letting out a breath, Josh nodded. "Okay, but here are the rules. Do exactly as you're told, both of you. Stay where you're told, both of you. Stay out of our way so no one gets hurt—not you two, not my coworkers."

Isabella softly said, "Or you."

His eyes landed on hers and his heart thumped furiously. He nodded and restrained himself from pulling her into his arms.

Swallowing he said, "Now, we need to get out of here and we need to assume they are watching us. We also need to assume they will follow us. So, for now, we go back into the U.S. and wait for Gaige to call."

Diego nodded and Isabella whispered. "Ok."

Picking his phone back up, he texted Gaige.

"Need to transfer all of Mateo's calls to my phone. Can we do this undetected? His phone has to stay here in his home."

He waited a moment, then a text came back.

"Yes. Activate his phone now and lay your phone next to it."

Following directions, Josh laid his phone next to Mateo's, then pushed the on button to light them up. He saw his phone receive information as a little circle turned on the screen. A few seconds later the word, "Complete" appeared quickly followed by a text from Gaige, "All set."

Pocketing his phone, he stepped past Diego and Isabella and walked out into the hall and to the living room. Pulling his gun from his ankle holster, he slid it into his front pocket, turned and saw Isi and Diego watching him from a few steps away. He nodded and Isabella walked toward him, Diego following closely behind. When the elevator doors opened, he looked inside, nodded for them to step in, then he stepped in and pushed the button for the garage.

His hand in his front pocket and on his pistol, he got his mind into work mode.

"Stay on either side of me and behind the walls of the elevator until I tell you it's clear."

"Okay," Isabella softly replied.

Diego simply said, "Roger."

The elevator slowed then came to a halt and Josh pushed the close-door button to keep them from opening. He stepped to the side where Isabella stood, blocking her from exiting and looked straight at Diego. He mouthed, "Ready?"

Diego nodded once. Kind of like their old military days. Assessing Diego for stress, he noted that at this point he seemed calm and not under duress. Josh needed him that way until they arrived at the hotel. Sending up a silent prayer, Josh pushed the open-door button and waited a heartbeat before looking out. Seeing no one in front of him, he slowly stepped off the elevator, looked around everywhere, then he held his left hand out for Isabella to take.

As soon as their hands met, he squeezed hers for reassurance then softly said, "Go."

Diego stepped out behind him and as if with a sixth sense, he could feel him behind them to the car. Letting go of Isabella's hand, Josh opened the car with the fob in his pocket, opened the door and pulled her inside by her hand. He kept his eyes on Diego as he walked the few steps to Josh's rental car. As soon as Diego reached the car, he looked back at Josh and nodded, then climbed in and Josh walked around to the driver's side of Isabella's car and got in, and locked all of the doors.

"I want you to scoot all the way down, as low as you can get, and put your hands over your head. Stay there until I tell you it's all right to get up. The streets are congested, and traffic is slower here in the city. It might take some time to get out, but that's when we are most vulnerable."

"Okay." He started the car as Isabella bent forward and put her hands over her head.

Then he eased the car from the parking spot and watched in his rearview mirror as Diego pulled the car out of the spot and drove up behind them. He then eased the car forward, turned right to exit the garage and pulled onto the street. Let the fun begin.

19

So many things ran through her mind. Her parents. Would they be safe? Eric and Cecily would hopefully get on a plane and out of La Quemada before anything happened and Emiliana would need to be in a safe place, hopefully with her parents. She worked remotely as a graphic designer, so she probably wouldn't suffer business hardships. Since her father's many businesses were her main clients, she'd be just fine if she didn't get caught up in Marco's potential crimes.

Josh calmly told her where they were. "We're back on Central Street. Soon we'll be able to move right along."

She closed her eyes and practiced even breathing. She'd never felt fear like she had when the faceless voice on the telephone said he'd come after her and cut her fingers off. What then? She'd never be a physician again. It was her life. Now, of course, she suddenly understood that all of the dangerous things going on in the world, things she'd heard and seen on the news, were real. She'd always felt removed from them. Now, she was in the middle of something not of her own doing, and yet, she was possibly running for her life. She worried her whole family also would suffer an awful fate because of Mateo.

Deep breath in. Slow breath out.

"We're turning off of Central and soon will be on the highway to the U.S. Diego is still behind us."

His driving was smooth, his breathing seemed even and steady and she wondered how he did it. Working in this type of profession must have its negative impacts.

"Okay, Isi, it's safe for you to sit up."

She slowly raised herself up so she didn't get dizzy, she took a few deep even breaths in and out and allowed her body to readjust.

Josh reached over and took her left hand in his right hand and squeezed. His energy, confidence and courage seeped into her and she felt better.

She turned her head to look at him. His profile was handsome. He was handsome. There were so many good qualities in him.

"May I call my parents and make sure they're all right and tell them what happened?"

"Yes. I'm happy to talk to them if they want."

She pulled her phone from her purse and was surprised to see her hands shaking as she did. Fisting and opening her hands to relieve some of the adrenaline that was likely the cause of her shaking, she took in a few more breaths, tapped her phone and located her father's number. Tapping his number, then the speaker icon, she listened as the phone rang.

"Mija, I'm so sorry I didn't see you before you left."

"Me, too, Papa. Is Mamá there and are you in a place where we can talk privately a moment?"

Her father hesitated then said, "One moment, Isi, let me get Mamá."

Movement then silence followed, then a door closed and another. She heard her father sit in his big leather chair in his office and smiled thinking of him sitting there.

"Okay Isi, Mamá and I are here. Are you all right?"

"Yes, I am fine. I'm with Josh and we are driving into the U.S. But, Papa, what is going on with Mateo? He is living in the middle of Nuevo Laredo, on the top floor of a complex. His furnishings are grossly expensive, far above what you pay him and so what he can afford. Italian suits, expensive trinkets and on top of it all, his phone is in the penthouse and his car is in the garage, but he is nowhere to be found. We answered a call that came into his office phone and the man on the other end said Mateo stole guns from him, which Mateo denies, but the man doesn't believe Mateo and he wants them back. He said in one day he would begin cutting off Mateo's fingers one each day and he would leave them on Mateo's desk in his penthouse. And he said, if we had Mateo's place watched, they'd come for me."

"Maldita sea - dammit, dammit, dammit." He could hear Bianca crying in the background.

Isi's voice cracked when she spoke again. "Papa, do you know anything about who he's been spending his time with?"

"I should call the authorities. No wait, can Josh hear this?"

Josh glanced at her then back to the road. "Yes, Mr. Martinez, I'm here."

"Josh, what do you think of this?"

"I think Mateo has gotten in trouble, either on his own or with others. I don't know what exactly he's been doing, but it has something to do with guns, and I've called my company to send help. They'll be in Texas later today.

Then we'll set up operations and begin tracking Mateo's moves. We could sure use something to go on though."

"I may have that for you. I added Tins tracking chips, to Mateo's wallet, shoes and car because he'd been in so much trouble. In case something horrible happened to him, I needed a way to track him down. In the past he'd gotten involved in drugs and I worried one of the cartels would come calling on him."

"Mr. Martinez, it would be helpful if you would send me the sign in and password information for that tracking device."

"I'll do it as soon as we hang up. Isi, send me Josh's phone number so I can send it to him directly."

"Yes, Papa."

"Josh." Mr. Martinez paused and Josh opened his mouth then closed it as soon as her father began talking again. "Whatever it costs, whatever you have to do, please find my boy. And, above all else, keep my daughter safe."

"Yes, sir, that's my plan."

The car began slowing down and Isabella looked out the windshield.

"Papa, I have to hang up, we're crossing the border now."

"I love you, Isi, you do what Josh says to do and stay safe. Call me with any information."

"Si, Papa. I love you and Mamá."

She tapped the end call icon and her heart thudded heavily. Fear and sadness were once again her companion and she hated it.

"I'll do everything in my power to keep you safe, Isi."

She turned and looked at him. This strong angel had been sent to her, and, for the first time, she wondered if this was God's master plan.

The border patrol agents were looking for something and you never knew if they were dirty.

"We'll likely be asked to get out of the car. Stay calm."

"Josh, I make this trip often, so it's all good."

"Sorry, I was in work mode."

She bit her bottom lip and he'd bet a million bucks she didn't mean it to be sexy, but it was. Sexy as fuck. He swallowed and looked forward at the patrol agents walking along the cars asking questions. Some folks had to get out of their vehicles, some didn't. As for him and Isi, they were two Hispanics going into the U.S., so it was likely they'd be asked to get out of the car. Diego, too. But then again, you never knew what they were looking for.

The closest agent motioned for him to roll down his window. Josh immediately complied.

"Sir, what is your purpose for entering the United States?"

"I live there. Currently staying in Texas but live in Indiana."

The agent looked him in the eye, then looked at Isabella.

"Ma'am?"

"The same. My parents live in La Quemada but I reside in Magnolia, Texas and we're going back to my place."

"How long were you in Mexico?"

"Just these past four days. My brother got married."

The agent looked them both in the eye, then nodded and walked along. Josh looked in his mirror and saw them question Diego and noted that after a few questions they kept on walking.

Soon the agents up ahead began letting the cars slowly move over the border and into the U.S. Once over the border, traffic moved faster and he felt more at ease that there wouldn't be an incident getting out of Mexico. They still didn't know who they were dealing with or why.

They had just crossed the border into the U.S. His phone rang and he pulled it from his pocket, tapped answer and the speaker icon.

"Masters."

"Josh, Hawk and Falcon will be there in three hours. Is your hotel secure enough?"

"I'm on my way there now. Not sure if there are rooms for everyone, but I also have Isabella with me and Diego. We'll need accommodations for five of us. I thought I'd look at an Airbnb or something."

"Roger."

"Also, Gaige, Mr. Martinez has Tin trackers on Mateo. He'll be texting me the username and password so we have a good lead on where Mateo might be, provided he still has the Tins on him. Wallet and shoes."

"That's perfect. Send it all through as soon as you get it, and we'll get working on it from this end."

"Roger."

"Out."

The line went dead, and a text came through soon after from Mr. Martinez. He handed his phone to Isabella.

"Can you read this text from your father and see if anything has to be replied to?"

"You trust me with your phone?"

He glanced over at her quickly, then back to the road. He couldn't help but grin.

"Absolutely."

She read the text then said, "It's the username and password. He then said, "Whatever the cost keep my children safe."

Josh nodded. "Reply, I'll give up my life to protect them."

"I'm not going to say that."

"Why not, it's true."

"You hardly know us. Why have you gone out of your way so much for my family?"

Looking into her eyes was no hardship. He'd look into them forever. That thought had his head jerking back slightly.

Once again with his eyes on the road he responded. "At first, I saw a very drunk groom and his dickhead friends trying to make him drink more than he should. It's clear Eric is not a big drinker. So, I couldn't help but step in. My friends and I partied with the rest of them, and for the most part, I just stuck close to Eric to make sure nothing happened to him. I also didn't know what kind of woman he had, but when you meet my sister, Jax, I measure all women by her. She's fierce. She's tough as nails and she takes absolutely no bullshit from anyone. She's a crack shot with a gun; she'll step into any fight. She's one of our top special operatives at the agency and she's also gorgeous on top of everything else. So, my thoughts were if Eric's future wife were anything like Jax, he was going to get an ass-kicking like he'd never seen before and I felt sorry for him again.

"Then he invited us to the wedding, and I felt that was a good way to make sure he was okay. And I met you. And the rest of your family. Besides Mateo, you seem like a wonderful family, successful in business, strong in your relationships and..." He swallowed. "I'm drawn to you, Isabella." He shrugged his shoulders. "I'm drawn to you."

He swallowed. "Then I kissed you."

He turned to look at her and he saw the softness in her eyes and the moisture that was gathering there.

"If life has taught me anything, it's taught me that it isn't forever. And if I hadn't learned that before now, today I have. Your life was threatened and I will not sit by and allow you to be harmed. I will not."

He glanced at her again and saw her swallow. She then lightly sniffed, and he tapped the turn signal to take the road where the hotel was located. He looked over at her again and she was still watching him.

"Tell him what you want to tell him," he said.

As he located a parking spot, Isabella typed out a response to her father on his phone. He parked the car and got out of his side. Walking to Isabella's door, he opened it and held his hand out for her.

When she looked up at him his heart thumped loud, hard and fast. When her hand grasped his, it was as if an electrical current shot up his arm and through his body. When she stood on her toes before him and touched her lips to his, he came undone. Life would never be the same as it was now.

21

She initiated the kiss. She had to. She was compelled to. His words, dammit, they dug deep into her. It was as if her soul or heart opened up in that moment and told her this was her future. He was her future. Now her resistance to him seemed foolish.

She didn't welcome the days to come. There were so many unknowns about the future. Mateo could get them all killed. Josh lived in Indiana and she lived in Texas. She was going to start her own clinic. She wanted to be where she could do the most good. He lived a high-risk lifestyle. Look what he'd done today. Calm. Sure. Brave. Strong. Every day he lived like that. Could she live that life with him? Could she live without him?

He looked into her eyes as if he were searching her soul or heart. Then he'd planted himself in there and he'd never leave. She knew it like she knew today was Sunday. It was exciting and it was frightening. The planned-out life she had for herself, well, shit, that was gone.

"We have to get inside, Isi."

"Yes." It came out all breathy and sexy and she didn't

even mean it that way. She just couldn't breathe right now. He'd cast a spell over her and she was hopeless.

He opened the trunk and pulled her suitcase out. When she reached for it, he chuckled and moved it away. Closing the trunk lid, he looked over at Diego, who strode toward them with a smirk on his face.

"Diego, can you check and see if they have rooms together at the end of the hall? We'll need three of them at a minimum, four if they have them."

"Sure."

"If it helps, I'll check out of mine and move into one of them."

"Okay."

Diego's eyes flicked to her and he smiled before preceding them into the hotel.

Isabella commented, "He's standing taller today. Something's different."

"I noticed that, too. He has a new goal in life I think."

They entered the hotel and he handed Diego a credit card. Then he took her hand and they walked to the bank of elevators.

As soon as the doors opened they stepped inside and she was relieved to see they were alone. An electric charge ran through both of them and when the doors closed; he turned quickly and pinned her to the wall. His arms wrapped around her. His lips consumed hers, and their breathing was the only sound in the elevator except their lips brushing lightly together.

As the elevator slowed, he nipped her lips one last time, then stepped back slightly as the doors opened. Another couple stepped in and he stood directly in front of her, to shield her. Protect her. Her heartbeat increased at the way he kept her safe. She'd never had anyone want to shield her life and it was an exhilarating feeling. She'd always thought of herself as a self-made woman. And she was. But this? Wow.

Her hands slid up his back and admired the breadth of his shoulders, the way his back then narrowed to his waist and she felt the solidness of the muscles beneath. He was magnificent.

He looked over his shoulder at her and she smiled but didn't stop her hands from roving over him.

The elevator slowed again, and she reluctantly moved her hands to her sides. The doors slid open with a whoosh and the couple in front of Josh stepped out of the car. Josh moved forward and stood by while she stepped in front of him as they, too, exited the elevator. His hand instantly took hers and he quietly led her down the hall. He stopped in front of a door, pulled a key card out of his pocket, waved it in front of the lock, and stepped back, allowing her to walk inside. As soon as she entered, the door closed. She turned and Josh stood before her, his eyes intense; his body beat a vibe that was totally intoxicating.

"You ready to finish what you started?"

Her heart hammered in her chest and the electric current that had been so present since the moment she met him sparked hot and wild. She swallowed to wet her dry throat, concerned she couldn't even say a coherent sentence. Her eyes locked on his and her skin heated with excitement.

"Yes."

He stepped forward and wrapped his arms around her, picking her up off the floor as his lips assaulted hers. His tongue delved deep into her mouth, consuming her.

His hands slid one at a time to cup her ass and pull her into his hardness.

Without thought she wrapped her legs around his hips. He walked them to the bed, placed a knee on the edge and lay her down in the center of it. He continued to kiss her mouth; his lips perfectly matched to hers. The power in his body, the controlled movements, the bunching and relaxing of his muscles, enveloped her.

He stood then and pulled his shirt over his head as his eyes locked on hers.

"Get undressed, Isi."

Her breathing came in spurts and the wetness between her legs increased. She unbuttoned her slacks as he unbuttoned his. She shimmied out of them as his hit the floor. She tugged at her light sweater and pulled it over her head as his briefs hit the floor. She lifted her head to look at him. All of him. He. Was. Perfect.

22

Her soft pink lacy undergarments contrasted (stunningly) with her olive skin-tone. Her dark hair spread out on the bed beneath her, framing her face, and her dark sexy eyes locked on his. He didn't know where to look. He wanted to stare at all of her.

Her breasts were firm, full, and still covered in delicate lace. His heartbeat pounded harder and he took a deep breath to temper his emotions. He wanted her. Desperately. More than he could remember ever wanting anyone.

"Remove your bra, Isi."

His voice didn't sound like his, rather, it was a deep growl filled with need.

She sat up and reached behind her. His eyes focused on her breasts; the instant she undid the hooks in the back, her breasts fell forward from the weight and his fingers tingled.

As she pulled the lacy bra from her body and her breasts came into full view, his eyes devoured them. This beautiful woman before him was a sight to behold. He wanted this moment imprinted into his brain forever.

Her graceful movements as she lay back onto the bed excited him. She was graceful now, but he wanted her hot, wrapped around him and begging him to come inside of her.

Unable to resist any longer, he reached forward and ran his hands up her bare legs. Her skin felt like satin under his hands, soft, warm, and pliable. He continued up her thighs until his thumb touched her center and her breathing hitched. His eyes quickly locked on hers and she licked her lips. Her nipples beaded tight and her breathing accelerated.

"You are gorgeous, Isabella Martinez."

"So are you, Josh Masters."

His thumb rolled over her clit as he watched the reactions on her face. Her hips rose so he added pressure. Moving under the fabric of her panties, Josh found her warm, wet center and massaged her as she moaned. He smiled as he watched her react to his touch. Tucking his fingers into the band of her panties he pulled them down her legs. Dropping them to the floor, he reached down quickly and pulled his wallet from his pants, nipped the condom from inside and opened the package.

Taking his cock into his hand, he pumped it a couple of times as he stared at Isabella sprawled out on the bed before him. She lifted her head and watched him stroke his shaft. Quickly rolling the condom on, he climbed onto the bed as her legs spread open for him. He kneed between her legs and hovered over her, his hands on either side of her body, his eyes boring into hers.

"Put me inside, Isi."

She moaned but leaned up and took his cock in her hand. She pumped up and down a few times which even with a condom felt amazing. His lips captured hers and she fondled him, her fingers grazing his balls, and then curling tightly around his cock and pumping again.

After a few times she lay back and placed the tip at her entrance. Her eyes opened to stare into his; a soft smile on her face showed her pleasure at what was about to happen.

His hips pushed forward, and he slid into her tight wetness; her heat wrapped around him, and his balls began to tighten. He moved out slowly and pushed back in. He wanted to enjoy this first time with her, but it wouldn't be his last. Every time he entered her; she lifted her hips, driving him deeply inside of her body. Her lips captured his and she whimpered into his mouth, pulling him into a spell, into her. He echoed her moans, trying without words to tell her they were now changed. They danced this dance together, each giving and taking. He rolled his hips against her, enjoying the feeling and the sounds of pleasure she made. She urged him to increase his pace, a pump and a roll and then it became a swift movement of them both furiously reaching for that pinnacle. Their skin heated, her body welcomed him, sucked him in and wrapped him tightly.

"Josh." She cried out and he moved faster.

"Josh. Oh God, Josh."

Faster he moved. He wanted to be there with her. She cried out as her body shuddered and he continued pumping, finally reaching that pinnacle and he let himself spill into her with a groan and a jerk.

He held himself above her body on his elbows, his breathing as well as Isabella's labored and their bodies damp from the exertion. He kissed her jaw, her ear, her neck; her hands wrapped tightly around his back, holding him close to her.

His phone began ringing and he hated the intrusion into this moment. He still had memories he wanted to permanently etch into his brain. The way she smelled, like a fresh spring breeze. The way she felt beneath him, the way their bodies fit together like two pieces of a puzzle. Her skin against his felt like the softest satin wrapping him in luxury, security and comfort.

Ring.

Her lips grazed the side of his face and his neck; he closed his eyes to memorize how they felt against his skin, the moisture and softness of her lips as they lovingly nipped along his skin.

Ring.

He let out a long breath. "I'm sorry, Isi."

"I hope you mean about the phone."

He pulled back and looked into her eyes. "Only that."

Pulling out of her body, he twisted and sat on the bed. Grabbing a tissue from the box on the nightstand, he handed it to Isi with a kiss to her lips. He grabbed another and pulled off the condom. Josh reached for the offensive phone. This better be good.

23

"Masters."

She watched Josh as he spoke to whoever had interrupted the most beautiful moment in her life. It. Was. Perfect.

"Okay. I'll pack-up. I'll call Shep and Travis and see if they want to join us, then we'll check out."

He tapped his phone then turned to look at her. His eyes roamed down her body with such heat in them she could feel the warmth. It was like he was actually touching her.

"You are the most gorgeous woman I have ever met Isabella Martinez."

She smiled. "Not to sound like a parrot, but you are the most gorgeous man I have ever met Josh Masters."

He reached over and softly cupped her breast, his thumb rolling over her rapidly tightening nipple.

"Your body responds to me. That's sexy."

She giggled. "How could it not."

Swallowing, he got serious. "Okay, I have to get to work at finding us a place to stay. There isn't enough room in the hotel. We'll need an Airbnb big enough for all of us. My teammates will be here in a little over an hour."

"How can they get here so quickly from Indiana?"

"We have a private jet. It gets us places quickly."

She sat up. "Your company has a private jet? How big of an agency do you work for?"

"There are eleven of us now. Plus Gaige's wife, Sophie, works with us sometimes, though they just had a baby, so I don't know how long that will continue. But she's great at research and she'll likely continue to do that. Jax came back to work as soon as the twins were three months old. Her husband, Dodge, works with us, too, so our mom is helping out.

"So, an agency with only eleven people can afford a private jet?"

He smiled and it hit all the yummy spots on her body. He likely didn't know how handsome he actually was.

"We make good money by working for high paying clients. We fill a need."

She took a deep breath; apparently real life was ending their brief but wonderful interlude.

"I have a girlfriend here in Escondido who might be able to help us out. She actually lives somewhere else and comes here occasionally to visit friends and family. She inherited the house, so she hates to sell it."

His eyes still captured hers. "We'll need sleeping accommodations for seven if Travis and Shep decide to join us. After all, I am here for Travis' wedding."

"I'm happy to share my bed," she purred.

He reached over and wrapped his arm around her waist and pulled her easily onto his lap. She straddled his body and felt him grow hard beneath her. That was so incredibly sexy. She wrapped her arms around his shoulders and stared into his eyes.

"You'll share your bed all right." He kissed her lips. "But you won't be sleeping much."

Isabella wriggled her hips and his thickening cock rubbed against her.

She continued to move back and forth on him and could feel the tip of his cock right against her. Lifting slightly, she could feel him stand completely at attention and she slowly slid down onto him. He groaned into her mouth. His hands moved to her hips as he rocked into her, seating her completely on him.

"You won't, either."

She began repeating their dance from earlier. It was good. They knew this rhythm instinctively. Sliding up and down on his length, she could feel every little nuance of how well he fit her. She could feel him slide inside of her and it felt fantastic. His hands on her hips, guiding her motions heightened her arousal. He knew what he wanted, too.

"Isabella, you are perfect."

He straightened and pushed his chest into hers, causing her breasts to rub deliciously against his pecs. The course hairs on his chest added a sensual abrading to her nipples and they responded by tightening. He began guiding her hips in a slight circle as she rose and fell, and her clit was massaged in the most delicious way. Her heartbeat thumped almost painfully within her and her skin dampened from exertion. Her nerve endings electrified her whole being in this erotic dance.

He lay back, but his hands on her hips kept her moving. His eyes fell on her breasts which were now bouncing and swaying and his nostrils flared and his jaw tightened.

He whispered, "Jesus."

She palmed each of her breasts and pinched her nipples and his hips began to raise and lower in time to hers. It sent him inside her further and she moaned.

"Let go, Isi."

She moved faster and ground against him and felt the fire grow wild and hot within her.

His desperation to reach the end could be heard when he called her name. "Isi."

She landed hard on him as her orgasm rushed forward. She meant to pull off him then, but he came instantly. She fell forward onto his chest, their hearts beating together against each other, their breathing rapid and deep.

"Jesus," he whispered again.

"Yeah," she managed.

"Fuck," he muttered.

"Yeah."

His arms circled her body and he held her close as they each regained their strength.

"We didn't use a condom," she whispered.

"No."

He kissed the shell of her ear, her jaw, her neck, then his teeth nipped at her neck.

She rolled off him and they both cleaned up. He looked down at her. "You started it."

She burst out laughing because she surely didn't expect that.

He shook his head, a grin on his face. Then he reached for his briefs and slid them up his legs. As he stood to pull them over his softened cock, his smile faded, and his eyes became serious.

"I'm clean."

She stared at him for a moment, her heart once again pattering away at his care and concern.

"I am, too."

He nodded and reached down to scoop up his shirt and pants. He leaned down and kissed her lips as she sat up. "But I'm not on birth control."

He froze for a split second, then nipped her lips again. "Neither am I."

She laughed then and enjoyed seeing his smile.

"Do you want to shower first, Isi or should I jump in?"

"You go, I'll take longer."

She watched his fine backside as he grabbed a duffle from the corner and walked to the bathroom. As the door closed, she flopped back on the bed and chided herself for getting more wrapped up in sex with him than being cautious. They'd need to be more careful moving forward. For crying out loud, she was a doctor, she knew better. But it was exciting and sensual and wildly sexy to throw caution to the wind with him. Still.

Huffing out a deep breath, she rose from the bed and walked to her purse on the desk and pulled out her phone. Dialing her friend Vanessa, she gathered her discarded clothing as the phone rang on the other end.

24

Josh finished his text to Hawk, giving him the address of their new location. The house fit their needs and was beautiful to boot. Spacious, it had sleeping accommodations for twelve, which, of course, was perfect. He opted for a bedroom with a king-sized bed, but not the master bedroom because that had doors onto a balcony. Keeping Isi safe was first and foremost and a balcony left it open to a security breach.

Instead, their bedroom, his and Isi's, had its own bathroom, but no outside access except for a couple of windows. Diego, Shep and Travis were sharing a room with bunkbeds, which they thought would be fun.

Isi was upstairs now, unpacking some of her bathroom supplies, and he came down to the second or middle floor, of the three-level home. The house had a full privacy fence around the property and a pool in the back for relaxing. During downtime they could enjoy some of the amenities. At least his friends could and that eased his guilt for working during his time which was supposed to be spent with Travis, Diego and Shep.

Pulling his laptop from its case, he logged on and then logged into the Tin website to check Mateo's tracking information.

It had been four hours since the phone call and that meant they had twenty left before Mateo's fingers would begin showing up on his desk. His phone rang and he saw Gaige's name on it.

"Masters."

"Josh, are you logged into the Tin site?"

"Yeah. It looks like he was tracked to an area of Nuevo Laredo, not terribly far from where he lives. But hasn't moved since then."

"Right. I called our computer genius, Jared, and asked him if there were a way to track body heat on these devices and he said there was. He worked at it and found that the body heat associated with Mateo's Tins had cooled about two hours ago."

"So, they either found the Tins and removed them or Mateo is dead."

Isi's gasp from the stairs caught his attention and he motioned for her to come to him. His laptop in his lap, phone to his right ear, Josh held his left arm out for her to sit next to him. She sat stiffly and he wrapped his arm around her shoulders and pulled her close.

"Yes. So, let's coordinate. Someone needs to go to the area and see if they can either find the Tins or if it's Mateo. You coordinate that. I'm appointing you lead on this mission. Also, we need to sort through Mateo's bank records to see if there were large deposits made recently to infer illegal activity. Can you find out where he banks?"

Isi nodded her head as she sat next to him and he kissed her temple.

"Yes."

She stood and walked across the room as she pulled her phone from her tan dress slacks.

"Papa," she said and he then went back to Gaige.

"Isi is getting that information from her family now."

"Okay, once we have this information buttoned-up, we can begin to trace Mateo's steps recently and who he was dealing with. From there, we should be able to locate him in the next few hours."

"Agreed. Hawk and Falcon are just a few minutes away. We'll secure the house we're at then set up and begin directing this mission."

"Wonderful. How is Diego doing?"

"Good. Actually, better than good. I think he feels a new sense of purpose. He applied for the retraining course Emersyn is in. How's she doing?"

"Keirnan said she's doing fantastic. She'll likely always have a limp, but she's excited about this training and expects to graduate in a month."

"Glad to hear it. I'll call in shortly. Mr. Martinez is willing to pay for this mission also. Any word from Casper on payment?"

"I haven't heard back. If we can show any involvement on this side of the border, he'll find the funds for it from our contact in the State Department."

"Good."

"Josh, how personal is this?"

His eyes darted to Isabella, standing across the room speaking to her father. Her eyes locked on his and held, and her lips slightly turned up into a smile.

"Very."

"Roger."

The phone went dead, and he searched the area in Nuevo Laredo where Mateo's Tins were located. They were only about two miles from Mateo's home. Zeroing in on the area, he could see a car chop shop, about three tattoo parlors, several bars, and two factories. Not the greatest area. So why would Mateo, with so much money running through his hands, decide to live there?

Isi came to sit next to him and held her phone up for him to see.

"Papa sent this. It's Mateo's banking information. Since he's on the company payroll, Papa knows at least this bank, which is where his salary is direct deposited."

Josh smiled at her. "You'll be an agent with us yet, Isi."

"No, I won't. And I'm happy with that."

A car pulled up outside and Josh leaned forward to set his laptop on the coffee table.

"Stay up here, Isi. It's probably either Hawk and Falcon or Diego, Travis and Shep, but just in case, follow the plan."

"Okay. If I hear commotion, I'm to run up and hide in the bedroom and call 911."

He kissed her nose then made his way down to the main level of the home. Looking out the windows to the driveway, he saw Hawk first. It was impossible to miss him; he was 6'8" and massive in size. Then he saw Falcon. A much younger version of his father, Ford. As they grabbed their gear and go bags from the back of the car, he waited until they began walking toward the house before opening the door.

"Good afternoon. May I help you?"

"Fuck off." Hawk growled then laughed. Falcon, who was more serious, like his father, pinched his brows together then shook his head.

Josh shook both of their hands then turned to lead them upstairs. "There are five bedrooms. I've taken one of the larger suites, without balcony access since I have Isi with me. Travis, Shep and Diego chose the room with the bunkbeds—they ran out for pizza—so the other rooms are yours to choose from."

Hawk walked past him, a grin on his face, then instead of stopping on the main level, he continued up to the third floor. Falcon followed silently behind. As the newest agent, most of this stuff was new to him, and Josh was grateful he wasn't trying to tell everyone how much he knew. That was hella annoying.

A key in the lock below had him looking down at the door. When it opened, Diego peered around the door, "It's us, Josh," he said.

Josh nodded and walked back to his laptop. The Tin account had updated and moved. Interesting for sure.

"Whatcha got for us?" Hawk boomed as he stepped off the bottom step, Falcon closely behind him.

"First, this is Isabella Martinez. Mateo Martinez is her older brother. Isi, Hawk and Falcon."

Hawk stepped forward and shook her hand; Falcon followed.

For the first time Falcon spoke up. "What do you have on the Tins?"

25

Isabella's phone rang so she stepped into the kitchen area. Though open to the living room, there still was some space so she wasn't interrupting the conversation of Josh and his coworkers.

"Hello."

"You only have eighteen hours before Mateo's fingers begin showing up on his desk at his place."

The call ended and she gasped. Her stomach lurched, her skin turned ice cold, and she began to shake.

Josh jumped up from the sofa and walked into the kitchen.

"Isi, what is it?"

"It was him. The man who has Mateo."

Josh pulled her into a hug and held her close. After a few minutes, he pulled away from her and looked her in the eye.

"We'll get him back. But for now, I need your phone to trace that call. I don't know how he got your number, but I'd guess he had Mateo's phone and now has all the numbers for your entire family."

"Oh, no. Mamá, and Papa."

"We'll get him. Let me look at your phone, then we'll figure out how to protect your family."

She nodded and took a deep breath.

He kissed her forehead and took her hand.

Walking to the dining room table where Hawk, Falcon and he had set up laptops, he handed her phone to Falcon. Josh pulled a chair away from the table and urged her to sit down.

Falcon pulled an electronic box from a duffle bag, then began connecting wires from the box to her phone.

"Falcon is tracing your call now. What we'll do then is see if the call is coming from an area close to where the Tin unit has been transmitting. We'll be able to get close to the location where Mateo is located."

She watched the men work. Hawk stared at his computer screen, Falcon pressed buttons and her phone beeped. He then watched his computer screen.

Josh rested his hand on her shoulder, his thumb gently moving back and forth. Hawk spoke first.

"Within a half mile radius of the Tin."

"Okay, let's go get him." Josh responded.

Immediately Hawk and Falcon began packing up their gear. Josh moved to leave but she grabbed his hand.

"Josh, you can't leave me here."

"I won't. I'll stay here with you in case this is a trap."

He walked to the coffee table and grabbed his laptop. Bringing it to the table, he typed a bit, then looked up at Hawk. "I'm in."

Hawk nodded and tossed his go bag containing his gear over his shoulder. Falcon followed behind him.

Josh then reminded them. "Comm units on. While en route, please."

Falcon gave him a thumbs up and Josh continued typing. He then took her phone, pried open the back of it and removed the battery. Pulling a phone from his bag, he turned it on, tapped some buttons and handed it to her.

"This is a burner phone. I pulled your family phone numbers from your other phone and dropped them into this one. Except Mateo's. So, please call your father and see if he knows a private security firm he can hire for protection. Don't tell him too much, we don't know if his phone is being bugged. Just ask if he has security and if not, can he get them."

She nodded woodenly. "He has security for the businesses."

"Do you know the name of his head of security?"

"Yes. Jonny Jay."

"Ask your father to call Jonny to come to the house and stay with the family and bring a couple friends."

"Okay."

She pulled up her father's number from the new phone Josh gave her and with shaking fingers, tapped her father's number.

Her father's voice was hesitant. "Hello."

"Papa, it's Isabella."

"Oh Isi. I've been so worried."

"Papa, listen. We can't stay on the line long and I need you to listen. Please call Jonny and have him bring some friends to sit at the house with you and the family."

"Isi, what..." Her father paused. "Okay. Yes, I see. I'll call now."

"I have to go, Papa. I'm fine I'm with Josh."

"Good. I love you, mija."

"I love you, too, Papa."

She tapped the end call icon and lay the phone down.

Josh then took the phone and pulled the battery. He handed her a new phone. "In case of emergency."

She nodded and Diego, Travis and Shep came downstairs.

Travis smiled. "We're hanging out at the pool. Come and join us."

Josh looked up at his friends. "Thanks, guys. Maybe in a while, I've got to man the computers for a bit while Hawk and Falcon are out."

Shep shook his head. "Man, you are all work and no play."

Josh laughed and looked over at Isabella. She knew exactly what he was thinking. They played. It was just sexier play.

Diego sat at the table in the chair Falcon had vacated as Shep and Travis walked outside from the patio doors.

"What's going on?"

"We've pinpointed an area where we believe Mateo is being held. Hawk and Falcon are on their way to rescue him."

"What can I do? I mean it, Josh. The more I think about getting back in some way, the more excited I get. Part of my problem with my PTSD is I was dwelling on it. That doesn't mean I don't need therapy or retraining or something. But, being useful is huge and that's the excitement of this type of work. Or what your boss's niece is doing."

The doctor in her couldn't help but jump in. "Diego, what have you done for your PTSD to date?"

"Man, it's just the bullshit stuff the VA allows. Not enough treatment to really help, but they did diagnose the PTSD. To get adequate treatment outside of the VA takes money that I don't have. My convenience store is doing okay, but it isn't flush enough yet to allow me the medical treatment that would help me out. Most of this treatment is out of pocket."

"I can help you find medical professionals that will help you, Diego. It's important for your quality of life to get treatment and there are programs that are available for little or no cost."

Diego took a deep breath and Isabella realized that focusing on Diego's issues kept her mind from what was going on with her family right now.

"Did Josh tell you about the program he knows of?"

"No. He didn't."

She looked at Josh for additional information. Instead, he pulled his phone off the table, tapped a few times, typed something in then handed it to her.

"My boss Gaige has a niece in this program. Emersyn was wounded in Afghanistan and is going through the program and retraining. I suggested Diego consider it."

Isabella looked through the program but her mind kept wandering to Josh. He was honestly a good person. Always trying to help others out. And her heart softened again for this handsome, strong, smart, sweet man. She'd be stupid to let him get away.

Josh saw the connection once Hawk and Falcon put their comm units on and connected to the GHOST system.

In the back of his mind, though, he was worried the kidnappers had already tracked Isi's phone and deliberated what their best course of action was here.

He typed their new action plan into the GHOST computer system and that Isi had been contacted by the kidnapper, what they were doing now and the plan if the house was breached. As Hawk and Falcon traveled, he finished setting up the security cameras around the house. They used battery operated cameras placed in windows and other rooms of the house to capture people coming onto the property, even through the roof, and inside various rooms in case they breached the outside. These were then connected to the GHOST servers so not only could he, Hawk, and Falcon watch from here, but at headquarters they were watching, too. Alerts would go out on their phones if a breach were detected.

Diego helped him around the house and Isabella sat

in a comfortable chair in a stream of sunlight reading about the retraining program he'd brought up to Diego. He glanced over at her and chuckled. She was absorbing the information and seemed impressed about it, based on some of her comments. Placing the final camera on the TV console, which looked like a small statue, he then went back to his computer and synced them all.

As he checked each camera function individually on his computer, Diego sat in a chair opposite Isi and asked her questions about the retraining.

"So, in the end the retraining is helping wounded veterans learn to ferret out and find child pornographers, kidnappers and traffickers?"

"Yes. The program first starts with the application, of course. Each veteran is then evaluated to find their strengths and weaknesses. From there, you're individually trained on the different systems they use based on your strengths. So, for instance, you're physically able to perform all the tasks you performed while in the service. But, your PTSD can be debilitating or hamper some of that if you have an episode. The first thing you'd be going through is a therapy program to help you cope with that. Then, you'd be trained on the systems they're using to locate kidnapped children, pedophiles, etc."

Diego rubbed his hands together and nodded. "I could do that."

Isi smiled at him. "You could, Diego, and it's very noble."

An alarm from his phone sounded and Isabella jumped up. "Josh, what's happening? Your phone has ALERT written across the screen."

He jumped up to grab his phone, then back to the computer. Watching the screen, he saw someone climbing onto the third-floor balcony outside using a rope ladder that had been tossed up and hooked onto the rail.

"Isi, we have a breach upstairs. Diego, I need you and Isi to stay here. Don't go anywhere."

Diego yelled, "Josh, I'm not armed."

Josh ran to his bag, pulled a 9mm from inside the zippered pocket, slid in a loaded magazine and racked the slide. "Are you sure you can handle this, Diego?"

"Yes."

Handing Diego the weapon, he looked at Isi. "Stay with Diego."

She nodded but said nothing.

Josh silently jogged up the steps, his phone in his hand so he could see the black-clad perp and where he was. Counting the rooms upstairs, there were two bedrooms each with their own bathroom. He guessed the perp was climbing in the bedroom window that Hawk had taken as his.

Listening outside the door, he heard a thud and then silence.

Quietly turning the doorknob, Josh cracked the door open but stood to the side in case the perp saw it move. When nothing happened, Josh listened again. Soft footfalls came toward the door. Standing back, he watched the door open slowly, but then heard Isabella scream.

The perp ran from the room just as Josh raised his gun hand and hit him on the back of the head with the butt of his gun. He tumbled down the stairs, falling noisily to the landing before it turned in a 45-degree angle to the second floor where Isabella was with Diego.

He then ran down as quickly as he could, jumping over the lifeless body of the perp, to the main floor living room. Another man with a full facemask held a gun to

Isabella's head, slowly walking her to the stairs that led to the ground level.

The fear in her eyes broke his heart. The assailant's left arm was wrapped around Isi's neck and shoulders, the gun at her temple. Diego stood across the room, shaking and frozen. Josh took a step toward Isi and the perp, but he warned, "Don't come near. She'll be a dead woman."

His heart pounded rapidly against his chest but his training kicked in. He backed up the four steps to where the other perp lay, grabbed him by the clothing on his shoulders and dragged him down the steps. He rolled down easily enough, and the mask he had on twisted. Josh held eye contact with the assailant who held Isi, and he reached down to pull the mask off the passed-out assailant.

Isabella gasped as she saw the man on the floor. Her attacker hauled her quickly with him to the steps. A shot rang out and the man holding Isabella jerked. It was enough for her to break free from his grasp and another shot rang out, knocking him to the ground.

Isabella ran to Josh and he quickly shoved her behind him. She grabbed the back of Josh's shirt but stepped out to his left slightly. "Diego, you need to take some deep breaths and slowly let them out," she urged.

His eyes darted to hers and held.

She reminded him, "In and out."

Josh looked over at Diego, still holding the gun he'd shot, just as Travis and Shep came running into the house from outside. Diego stood frozen in place, his eyes focused on Isabella

"Diego. Lay your weapon down." Josh yelled.

He began breathing and slowly lowered his weapon.

Josh went to the perp Diego had shot and checked for a pulse. It was faint, but he had one.

Josh's phone rang and he answered it. "Masters."

Gaige asked, "What's happening?"

"Two assailants breached the house one from upstairs, one down."

"Okay, I'm looking at the cameras. The upstairs camera didn't sync. The downstairs camera doesn't show an assailant."

"This all happened as I was syncing. Either bad timing or they were watching and knew the lag time in the syncing process."

He looked over at Isabella and waved her over to him. Shep went to Diego and gently took the gun from him, unloaded the gun and lay it on the counter. He then grabbed a bottle of water from the refrigerator and opened the top, setting it on the table in front of Diego.

Josh wrapped his arm around Isabella and walked her to the table. Pulling out a chair, she sat, and he sat in the chair next to her. He looked over at Shep and angled his head to the men laying on the floor while pulling up the computer screen with the cameras on it.

Speaking to Gaige, Josh said, "All cameras are on now. Did you resync them?"

"Yes. Call local authorities and deal with your men there. Call me if you need any help with them. I'll patch into Hawk and Falcon and let them know you're tied up."

Isabella studied Diego. Her emotions were all over the place. The fear, while still present, was beginning to leave her body. She inhaled deeply for three seconds, held it and exhaled for three seconds; soon she started to feel her normal self again.

"Diego, thank you so much for saving me."

"I almost didn't, Isabella." His voice shook. His eyes looked in her direction, but weren't focused clearly yet.

"But you did."

Josh took the pulse of the man laying at the bottom of the steps. Then he pulled his phone up and tapped a few times.

"I need the police and an ambulance to come to 13345 Waverly Beach Road. One man is shot and one man is unconscious."

Once she knew Diego was okay, she wandered over to the man who'd been shot. As she knelt beside him Josh barked, "Isi no, don't."

"I have to Josh, I'm a doctor."

Josh rushed over and knelt beside her. "I'll be here in case he comes to and tries anything."

Examining for bullet wounds, she found one had hit him in the leg and one in the side. His breathing was labored, and bubbles were forming at the site of the bullet hole.

"His lung is leaking into his chest. I need to watch him closely to make sure his lung doesn't collapse. Please help me turn him to the left lateral recumbent position then we'll need to get a tourniquet on his leg."

"I know that means to turn him onto his left side, but if I'm to help you, you'll need to tell me in layman's terms."

She nodded as she held her hand over the wound as much as she could and put her ear to his chest.

"I can hear gurgling and his breathing becoming shallow."

Sitting back, she examined his chest and saw one side bulging.

Placing her hands over the wound, she spread it open and allowed air to escape from inside the chest wall. Sirens in the distance told her an ambulance was on its way.

The hissing sound decreased as did the bulge in his chest. She kept her hand on his chest and glanced over at the unconscious man, Dominic Juarez, being watched by Travis across the room. Travis kneeled beside him and felt for a pulse, and nodded to her when he caught her watching.

Josh asked her. "You know him?"

"Yes. He's a friend of Mateo's. Why would he be trying to kidnap me?"

"How close are they?"

She shook her head. "Sadly, not that close if he has something to do with Mateo's disappearance."

The sirens sounded in the driveway and Shep walked downstairs to open the door for the ambulance and police. Her hands still shook slightly after everything that had gone on, and now having to go through it all again with the police was an unpleasant thought, but necessary. She took a deep breath and let it out slowly.

As the paramedics rushed upstairs, she began relaying what was happening to her patient.

"He has a hole in his right lung. It was leaking air into the chest wall so I spread it open to allow the air to release. He also has a bullet hole in his leg."

The paramedics rolled him over and began administering fluids, checking vitals and stabilizing his condition. Once he was stable, they lifted him onto a gurney now folded on the floor. Raising the gurney, they wheeled him to the steps and slowly carried him downstairs. Within seconds, a second EMT crew came to work on Dominic.

She watched, slightly detached from the whole scene, and wondered, for about the millionth time, what Mateo had gotten into that his friend tried to harm him and then tried to kidnap her.

Josh gently nudged her toward the kitchen. He stepped around her and turned the water on in the sink, letting it warm, then he sweetly took her hands in his and ran them under the water, removing the blood on them.

"Are you all right, Isi?"

The softness in his voice and the concern in his gorgeous brown eyes made her tear up. She sniffed as daintily as she could and blinked her eyes rapidly to stop the tears flowing.

She nodded, afraid conversation at this point would simply have her sobbing like a baby.

"We need to speak to the police to explain what happened. Then we need to figure out why Mateo's friend is involved in kidnapping and gun trafficking."

"Okay." It came out as a whisper.

The echo of footsteps on the stairs caused her to turn her head. Josh handed her a towel to dry her hands then took it and dried his own.

Josh walked toward the two police officers.

"I'm Josh Masters. It was my gun used to shoot one of the assailants." He raised his hands and tucked them behind his head, and she noticed his friends all did the same thing. One of the officers looked into the kitchen and stared at her. "Show me your hands."

Dropping the kitchen towel she'd picked up from somewhere, she raised her hands, a new fear filling her stomach and body. She'd never in her life been in this position.

She kept her eyes locked on the police officers. The one who initially spoke to her then walked toward her. "Do you have any weapons on you?"

"No, sir," she managed.

"I'm going to check, all right? You keep your hands raised."

"Okay."

He patted her legs, her hips and waist then one by one had her drop her arms and he gently pressed along her arms looking for weapons.

"Okay, please take a seat on the sofa and remain there while we clear these men."

It seemed an eternity before the weapons had been cleared and the men divested of any of their weapons. It took another hour or more for Josh to explain what happened, show the officers his computer system still set up on the table and what he did for a living. To say you could hear a pin drop as his friends—and she—absorbed his information would be a total understatement.

Josh was impressive as he spoke calmly to the officers, gave one of them his boss' phone number for any additional information and made sure they understood his mission here.

Josh asked, "Can you hold the two men in the hospital until I or my co-operatives are able to question them further about Mateo?"

"I'll call my Chief. Should I run this all through you or through your boss?" the officer asked.

"You can run it through either of us. I'm lead on this mission, but if your Chief needs anything from a higher up, Gaige is in contact with the State Department and we can get clearance from them if need be."

State Department? The full picture was forming in her mind of just what Josh did for a living and her body instantly felt cold.

It was another hour after the police left before Josh was able to answer all of the questions from Travis, Shep and Diego. Isabella sat quietly as they all talked and he worried about her stillness.

"Look guys, I can answer more questions later, but right now I've got a few things going on here. I have to check in with Hawk and Falcon to see how they're doing with finding Mateo and I've got to see if his bank records are finally available so I can begin figuring out what he was into. Can we pause this conversation until after dinner?"

Shep nodded and Travis stood, shook Josh's hand and his head. "I always knew you and Jax were different in some respects, Josh. Your secretiveness is understandable now and relieves all of my anxieties about why you would be gone for such long periods. 'Security'"--Travis used air quotes here--"just seemed too tame for some of the things I'd heard over the years. You have my respect and admiration."

Relief washed over him. "Thanks, Trav. I hated having to be so secretive to my friends, but we're called GHOST for a couple of reasons, one of them being, we need to fly under the radar. We fill a need, and we can't keep doing that if everyone knows about us."

"Understood." Travis walked away from the table. "So, I'm going to take a nap then tonight I'm making a huge dinner for everyone."

"Deal."

Travis and Shep walked upstairs and Josh turned to look at Diego. "You okay, man?"

Diego nodded. "I know I froze up when those men broke in and took Isabella. It was not expected, and I was not prepared, though I thought I was. But..." He hit his chest with his fist. "Respect." He cleared his throat then said, "I'm going to try and enter the therapy program and retrain as an agent to help those kids, man."

Josh smiled at his friend. He reached over, grabbed Diego's hand and shook it vigorously. "I'm proud of you, Bud. So, fucking proud of you."

Diego's eyes welled with tears. He nodded and walked to the steps to join Travis and Shep.

Josh sat next to Isabella, who was still very silent through all of this, and turned his chair to face her at the table.

"Hey. You've been awfully quiet. Will you talk to me?"

"Yes." She faced him, her features, while still incredibly beautiful, were set in a serious expression.

"Do you have any questions, Isi?"

She inhaled deeply and let it out in a slow whoosh. "Did you really come here for Travis' wedding or are you investigating my brother?"

He tucked her hair behind her ear, enjoying the feel of

her silky strands between his fingers. "I'm here for Travis' wedding. The rest is partly job hazard in that I am a civilian special op and helping people in situations like this is what I do, and partly a blessing because I met you."

Her eyes locked on his and held.

He took her hands in his and squeezed gently. "Were you worried that I was playing you?"

She nodded, her eyes glistening with tears.

He smiled softly at her. "No, querida, I was not and am not playing you."

He motioned between them. "This, here, is genuine. It's also a complete surprise to me. I've never in my life felt about someone the way I feel about you. You've taken me completely off-guard and turned me inside out."

A single tear slid down her cheek and he quickly swiped it away with his thumb. Then he slowly dipped his head and kissed her soft, full lips.

She kissed him back and his heart felt happy again. He realized he'd been worried as her silence continued.

He leaned back and looked into her eyes.

"I have to get to work for a while. Do you want to sit here with me or do something else?"

"I'd like to sit with you. Maybe there's something I can do to help."

He kissed her forehead. "There just might be. We have to go through Mateo's banking information and see if we can find unexplained large deposits, then find a pattern or trace where these payments have come from."

She smiled. "I can help with that."

He stood and she followed. Walking to the other side of the table where his computer was set up, he began typing information into the GHOST system.

"Ah, Mateo's records have been uploaded to our

system." He clicked and opened a few of the documents then turned and pulled another laptop from his bag on the floor.

Opening it up, he typed in his username and password and turned it so Isi could see it.

"This is a folder I just opened for you. It contains Mateo's bank records. Start with the most recent and work back. So, we're looking for large deposits that are not his payroll deposits. Then, I'll start a spreadsheet for you to enter the information into so we can look for patterns."

"Okay."

She clicked on the folder and opened one of Mateo's statements and immediately got to work. His heart swelled with pride watching her get at it after all she'd been through.

Turning to his own computer, he pulled up his emails and opened one from Gaige.

"Mateo has been moved. Hawk and Falcon found evidence of someone being tied to a post, blood, and hair at one of the locations they searched. An old factory. They're on their way back now."

It was sent an hour ago, which meant they'd be back in about an hour.

"Isi, they didn't find Mateo."

She stopped looking at his records and sat back. "Did they find a finger?"

"They're coming back, we can ask them then, but the report doesn't say anything about an appendage being found. We still have a few hours to go."

His phone rang and he quickly answered it.

"Masters."

"This is Chief Dunning from the Escondito Police

Department. We've just been informed that the two men you requested to interview are now awake and able to answer questions. My officers will meet you at the hospital if you want to question them."

"Thank you. Yes, I'll be there in thirty minutes."

Isabella grabbed her purse. "I want to go with you, Josh."

"Are you sure, Isi?"

"Yes, I'm sure. I want to know why Dominic was trying to kidnap me and where Mateo is and how he's involved. And, for God's sake, why all of this was going on?"

"You know he may not want to answer those questions."

Taking a deep breath, she tried remembering the last time she'd seen Dominic before today. He'd been somewhat flirty but overall, happy. He and Mateo had just been planning for their own business venture.

"I just remembered, the last time I saw Dom, he said that he and Mateo were going in together on a new business venture."

"Do you know what kind of business?" She shook her head and he nodded. "I'll just run up and tell the guys we're leaving so they don't worry."

She watched him go up the stairs then pulled her

burner phone from her pocket and dialed her father's number.

The phone rang a few times and her stomach knotted up. As soon as he answered relief flooded her body.

"Hello."

"Papa, it's Isi. I have a different phone for right now. How are you and Mamá?"

"We're fine Isi. Jonny is here with two of his men. Eric and Cecily have postponed their honeymoon for a couple of days so that we can make sure they are here and protected. Emiliana is still here as well. Are you safe, Isi?"

"I am now. We had a close call a while ago. Papa, what kind of business did Mateo and Dominic Jaurez get into together?"

"It had something to do with cars I think. Dominic has some contacts in the States, and he was going to find them cars to buy so they could fix them up and resell them."

"Are they still doing that?"

"As far as I know. Why all of these questions, Isi?"

She hesitated then took a breath. "Two men broke into our house here in Escondido and tried to kidnap me. One of those men was Dominic Juarez."

"Oh my God, Isabella. Are you hurt? Where was Josh? Where are you now?"

"Papa, Josh is here, and he and Diego stopped the kidnapping. I'm fine now. I was shaken up before but, please don't worry. Josh has this under control more than you know."

"Mija, maybe you should come back home here to stay with us under Jonny's protection."

Josh came running down the stairs, his eyes locked on her. From this vantage point, she saw the full impact of Josh Masters. Strong, virile, handsome, agile and oh, so sexy. Plus, she felt safer with him than she ever would with anyone else.

"No, Papa, I'm safe here."

Josh stood before her, staring into her eyes. It warmed her from head to toe.

"Please be careful, Isi. We love you."

"I love you, too, Papa. Mamá, Emi, Eric and Ceci as well." She moved to end the call but remembered one more thing. "Oh, Papa, did they have a name of this business?"

"Yes. It's a play on their names. MatDom. They created a limited liability company in the U.S. for it."

"Thanks, Papa. Stay safe."

She ended the call but continued to look into Josh's clear brown eyes. They were expressive eyes. But when she looked deeply into them she saw the whole person.

"Mateo and Dominic started a company together called MatDom. Something to do with cars."

Josh's brows furrowed briefly, then his forehead smoothed out. "I'll have Hawk and Falcon look into it." He sent off a text then took her hand. "Let's go before the police change their minds."

He looked out the door before ushering her to the car. Closing her door, he walked around the front of the car, but he was completely vigilant, looking all around for any signs of danger.

Climbing into the driver's seat he pushed the button on the dash and started the car. Grabbing his seatbelt, he buckled up and waited for her to do the same. His phone rang and he pulled it from his pocket and answered it on speaker.

"Masters."

"It's Hawk. MatDom, LLC is a valid limited liability

company. Organized in Texas two years ago. It says the purpose is buying and selling cars. There's a Texas address listed here."

"Do you and Falcon want to head over to that address and see what you find? Isi and I are headed to the hospital to interview the two intruders. One of them is Dominic Juarez of MatDom."

"Roger. Dominic is listed as the registered agent of MatDom."

"I'll contact Gaige and see if headquarters can run a bank records check on MatDom. We may get more information that way."

"Roger. Out."

The line went dead, and she turned to Josh as he pulled from the driveway.

"How would cars get a person in trouble?"

Josh shrugged. "There are so many things that can happen. Theft. Title fraud. Straw buying."

She thought about it a minute. "I understand theft. I don't understand the other two."

"So, I'm wondering what the intent of this business was in the beginning. I'd doubt, but I'm not sure, Mateo would get involved with theft. Not intentionally because they created an LLC. To go that far for a bogus business seems stupid at best. But, title fraud is a way to grab some easy cash. You agree to sell a car for someone on consignment. They bring you their vehicle and you ask them to sign the title so there's a smoother transaction. Then, you sell the car and don't give the actual owner the money for the sale. They've already signed the title, so what is their recourse? Especially if it's a cash transaction."

"Oh. Wow, people actually do that?"

He chuckled. "Isi, you'd be amazed at what people actually do to others."

"What is a straw-buyer then?"

"That's kind of what I'm thinking Mateo was involved in. Let's assume they were doing this. MatDom buys cars from people here in the U.S. They load them up into containers of some sort and transport them into Mexico. That way they avoid tariffs and taxes. It seems like a victimless crime, except for the government, right? The seller makes money on the sale, then they transport them to Mexico and sell them and the buyer gets a title and a vehicle. The loser is the government and state where the purchase is made because the tariffs on imported goods aren't paid."

She twisted to look at him. "Why would they get involved in something like that?"

He shrugged. "They could sell the cars for the same price they'd normally have gotten but make more money because they aren't paying tariffs. Money. It's usually the root of all evil."

Her brows bunched together. It seemed like a stupid risk to take for the small amounts of money they'd make on each car. Unless they were transporting huge numbers of cars. Josh picked up his phone and tapped a couple of times. Setting the phone in the cupholder, she listened as it rang.

"Hawk."

Josh responded. "Hawk, I have something else for you to check out."

Josh turned into the parking lot of the hospital.

"Yeah, go ahead," Hawk replied.

"The area that Mateo lives in is very industrial. I'm wondering if there's a place that is doing a ton of shipping in that area. Perhaps large shipping containers that could hide cars."

"We'll check it out."

"Thanks. Out."

Parking in a spot not far from the entrance, he unbuckled his seatbelt and got out of the car. Walking around to the passenger side, he saw a car pull in two rows back with two men in the car. He made eye contact with the driver and that ugly feeling crawled all through his body. Grabbing his phone, he redialed the number for the chief who'd called him earlier, Chief Dunning.

"Chief Dunning."

"Chief, this is Josh Masters. Isabella Martinez and I just arrived at the hospital. I'm calling to confirm we can go right in."

He stopped and stared at the driver, who held his gaze

for a moment, then busied himself with something in his console.

"Yes, Mr. Masters, you can come right in."

"Confirmed. Do you have security by their rooms?"

"Yes. Both men have security details. Why do you ask?"

"I just arrived at the hospital and a car followed me into the parking lot and is now sitting and watching me exit the vehicle."

He opened the door for Isabella, nodded to the car behind them, then quickly ushered her along with his hand on her back to the entrance.

"I'll have an officer stop by the hospital and guard the entrance just in case this is related."

"Thank you Chief."

Josh ended the call and hustled Isabella along to the entrance. Inside, he stepped to the windows on the right and watched the car to see if the occupants were exiting.

The driver's door opened first, then the passenger side and both men hopped out of the car. They walked slowly along the cars, stopping to pay close attention to Josh's rental. Pulling his phone up, Josh recorded them looking at his car. Then one of them dropped to the ground. A minute later, he popped back up and Isabella gasped.

"What did he just do?"

Josh quietly responded. "Either a tracker or a bomb. I'm hoping for tracker, but to be on the safe side, I'm sending this video to the Chief and to headquarters."

The two men then turned and got back into their car. Stopping the video, Josh snapped a few pictures of the car and the two men inside. He couldn't see the license plates but just then a police cruiser pulled up. Thinking this was a good thing, Josh went outside to speak to the officer.

"Hello Officer. My name is Josh Masters. I was just on the phone with Chief Dunning."

The officer stepped from the car and Josh saw his badge "Hodge".

"Officer Hodge." He pointed to his badge.

Pulling up his phone, Josh showed him the video, then pointed to the car and the two men inside. They quickly backed from their parking spot and squealed out of the parking lot. Sort of a tell right there.

Officer Hodge grabbed his radio and called out the car's description and asked dispatch to send available units to find it. He then called in the bomb squad.

"If you want to go up and question the suspects, I'll call you if we find anything Mr. Masters. But, before you leave the hospital, make sure you've spoken to me or the Chief to make sure your car is fine."

Not sure which was the right decision, he decided to go up to question the two men first and deal with the car later. If they had to get a driver to come and take them to the house, he'd do that. It was a rental and nothing of value inside of it anyway.

Stepping onto the elevator with Isabella, his hand held hers tightly. Thoughts of something happening to her sent a chill down his spine. Not on his watch. Actually, not ever. He'd defend her till his dying day. Which was a sobering thought.

His phone rang and he saw Jax's name on the read out. He chuckled, showed the phone to Isi and answered it on speaker.

"Hey sis. How are my perfect niece and nephew?"

"Perfect." She sighed. "At least they are now, they're sleeping. Honest to God Josh, I've never seen so much puke, shit, piss and spit in my entire life. It's a damned good thing I love these little shitters because otherwise, gross."

He laughed and so did Isabella.

"Are you with someone?" Jax asked.

"Yes. Isabella Martinez, meet my sister Jax Sager. Jax, Isabella. Doctor Isabella Martinez."

"Doctor? Are you hurt? What the hell is going on there? Gaige filled me in a little bit. Dodge filled me in more. You went down for Travis' wedding and what the hell did you step into Josh?"

He took a deep breath. "Okay, slow down. So, first of all, Isi and I are in the hospital to question the two men who tried to kidnap her. Local PD is doing us a favor. After that, I have to talk to the officer downstairs who is investigating whether or not there's a bomb on my car. Then, I'm hoping Hawk and Falcon can find some shipping containers which will help to pull this puzzle together. After that, we're hoping to find Isi's brother, Mateo. Then, Travis is getting married in four days. How's that for a vacation?"

He looked down at Isi and felt bad that a sadness had fallen over her. He'd been trying to alleviate Jax's worries by joking and it made Isi sad.

"Shit. You get all the fun. Next time, I'll go on vacation and you can have Uncle Josh duty."

He laughed, squeezed Isabella's hand and winked at her. That made her smile.

"Deal."

"So, am I going to meet Isabella in person?"

He looked at her face. The perfection that stared back at him made him want to yell, "Yes." Because not only was she physically gorgeous. She was everything a man could want in a partner.

"I hope so." Was all he could say.

The elevator doors opened, he looked up at the floor number, then he and Isabella stepped out.

"So, Jax, we're just about to walk into the room, can I call you later?"

"Yeah. Be careful Josh. I can't lose you. Comprende? It was nice kind of meeting you, Isabella."

"It was nice kind of meeting you too, Jax." Isabella smiled and his heart hammered.

"I'm careful. I love you sis. Kiss my niece and nephew for me. Hi to Dodge."

He turned them down the hall and led them to the rooms at the end of the hall where two armed officers stood.

31

Isabella's heart raced the closer they got to the rooms at the end of the hall. Taking a deep breath and letting it out slowly, she readied herself for...what? She wasn't sure what she was preparing herself for. Except maybe that Mateo was already dead. Her brother irritated the shit out of her but she loved him and didn't want him dead.

Stopping in front of the officers at the end of the hall, Josh introduced them.

"Josh Masters and Dr. Isabella Martinez to speak with Dominic Juarez and his partner in crime."

"Yes, Carlos Mendoza." The officer to the right responded.

"May we speak with Dominic Juarez first?"

Josh looked down at her for confirmation and she nodded. Her nerves had begun to take over and she worried that she wouldn't be able to say anything. She'd worked for three years in the trauma center of a large hospital before she'd been hired at the clinic she now worked at. She'd dealt with all sorts of horrible situations with speed and efficiency. But none of those were personal. This now, this was personal and she was worried she wouldn't be able to handle it well. But, she knew Josh could. That helped her anxiety subside. That, and he squeezed her hand again. A silent message that he was here with her.

Turning to the left, the officer opened the door first and looked at Dominic laying on the bed.

"I'll be leaving the door open during your visit. He's restrained so you don't have to worry, but just in case, all you need to do is let me know you need assistance and I'll be right there."

"Thank you, Officer." Josh responded. Isabella simply smiled at the officer and he smiled in return.

Stepping into the room, the familiar beeping of the heart monitor and the smells of alcohol and medicinal supplies weirdly calmed her. This was her element.

Nearing the bed, Dominic's eyes landed on hers and held. She refused to look away which made him nervous as his eyes began darting between the two of them.

Josh started. "Dominic Juarez, I'm here to question you on your involvement in the attempted kidnapping of Isabella Martinez. Why did you try to kidnap her?"

Dominic simply sneered.

"Let me try again. What is your involvement in the disappearance of Mateo Martinez?"

Josh let go of her hand and crossed his arms over his massive chest. It made him look menacing. Imposing. Wild. Exciting. Her heart fluttered at the figure he made.

"Mateo has created his own mess." Dominic finally replied.

"In what way?"

"He stole from someone who doesn't handle people

stealing from him well." Dominic's lips tightened and he began fidgeting slowly with the blanket covering him.

"Who did he steal from?"

"Who did he steal from? That's a great question. I'd like to know if he's stolen from me in the past, too."

Josh stepped forward a half step. "You didn't answer my question. Who did he steal from?"

Dominic straightened himself in his bed and avoided eye contact. He didn't want to answer these questions and he was determined to avoid answering them at all cost. She looked up at Josh. "He's lying and not going to give us good answers. Why don't we try and make a deal with Carlos? He'll likely be more eager to cut a deal for no jail time than this traitor."

"I'm not a trait…"

Isabella began walking to the door but Dominic said no more. Josh followed her out and they both stopped in front of the other door. The second officer opened it up and looked inside. Carlos had been shot twice so his condition was more serious.

Walking to the foot of the bed, Isabella picked up his chart and looked it over.

"Surgery to repair the bullet hole in his lung and side. Bullet extracted. A second bullet extracted from his calf. No lasting damage other than the anticipated scar tissue. He's on meds that make him tired, but that can also pull down his resistance to questions. Though, whatever he tells us we'll need to take with a grain of salt. He may also be impaired slightly."

Josh looked into her eyes and nodded. They stared at each other for some time; it was comforting. She could see him. Him. The man. His eyes weren't shifting back and forth. He wasn't trying to avoid looking at her. He seemed to want to look at her. To see her. Her.

She swallowed to wet her throat. Her heartbeat sped up. Josh opened his mouth to say something, then stopped. Instead he winked at her and if he only knew what that did to her, he'd have ammunition for an eternity to stop any argument they'd ever have.

He then turned to Carlos. "Carlos, my name is Josh Masters and I'm here with Isabella Martinez to question you about your attempted kidnapping of Isabella Martinez. Why were you trying to kidnap her?"

His dark eyes darted between the two of them, but he didn't move his body. He was likely sore at this point, which was good for them.

As she watched him though, she remembered the snarl on his face as he jumped at her and grabbed her while Diego was facing Dominic. She could only see his mouth and eyes but that was enough. She'd likely have some trouble sleeping in the next few days remembering his expression.

"Where is Mateo Martinez?"

"Warehouse."

It came out weak, but she heard it. Warehouse.

"Which warehouse?" Josh continued.

"The Plástico house."

"Where is that?"

"Nuevo Laredo."

"Who is holding him?" Josh leaned down to look directly into Carlos' eyes.

Carlos tried taking a deep breath but he winced as a pain shot through him and halted while he caught his breath. Josh continued to stare down at him and Isabella's doctor kicked in seeing a patient in distress. She started to say something but then Carlos said, "Tony."

"Tony who?"

Carlos swallowed. "Morales."

Josh then softened. "Why are you telling me this? Aren't you worried that you'll be outed?"

"Is Dominic still alive?"

"Yes."

"Then I'm already dead."

32

Josh shook Carlos' hand. "Thank you for helping."

Carlos grunted and said nothing else. Josh grabbed Isi's hand and turned to leave the room.

As they stepped out, Josh stopped to talk to the two officers who were still guarding the end of the hall.

"Carlos believes Dominic will kill him. Not sure if he'll try it here but it's likely if he gets loose, he will."

"Thank you, sir." The officer on the left replied.

Josh then turned and put his arm around Isabella's shoulders as they walked to the elevator. Reaching forward to push the down button, he kissed the top of her head and pulled out his phone. "Are you okay Isi?"

She looked up at him and smiled, though it didn't reach her eyes. "Yes. Do you have enough information?"

"Let's find out."

He dialed Hawk's phone and the elevator doors opened. Waiting for Isabella to step on, he followed her in, grateful they were alone.

"Hawk."

"Are you still in Nuevo Laredo?"

"Just left. We're going to need your help. There's a lot to cover and not enough time to do it. By my calculations, Mateo only has three more hours before he starts losing fingers."

"Yeah, that's about what I figured for time too. I did get some information. I have to make sure my car hasn't been wired with a bomb before I can run down. We're looking for a plastics factory or a place called the plastic house. Something like that."

"Roger. We'll start looking. Stay in touch."

"Roger."

He hung up the phone and tucked it in his pocket. "I have to run back down to Nuevo Laredo and help Hawk and Falcon search for Mateo."

"I want to come with you."

"No, Isi, it might not be safe. I don't know what I'll be dealing with and I don't want anything to happen to you."

She turned to face him, her hands on his chest, her eyes locked on his. "If you find Mateo and he needs medical assistance, I'm the best one to help him."

"Isi..."

"No. Josh. I'm going with you."

Staring into her eyes, so many thoughts ran through his mind. She's tough. Jax was going to love her. She's smart. She's caring. She's gorgeous beyond belief. Jax was going to love her and he'd already fallen. He swallowed as he ran that last thought through his mind again. He'd already fallen in love with her. Shit.

"Isi, I can't let you get hurt."

"I'll stay out of the way, I'll do what's needed. But, I'm going."

The elevators opened to a throng of onlookers crowding at the windows, effectively blocking the hallway.

A quick glance out the windows confirmed the bomb squad was outside and a large section of the parking lot was roped off and secured. Holding Isabella's hand tightly, Josh pulled her along behind him as he made his way through the crowd. He walked over to the bomb squad officer and pulled his wallet from his back pocket. As he showed his ID he asked, "Find anything on my car?"

"A tracking device. But the bomb squad wanted to make sure there wasn't anything else so they're looking it all over carefully. We'll need your video for our records and we'll need you to come down to the station to make a statement."

"Can the station visit wait for a few hours? I've got an emergency."

The officer looked into his eyes, then looked at Isabella.

"Please officer, it has to do with my family."

The officer blew out a breath. "It shouldn't be a problem. Make sure you show up though." The officer then pulled a card from a holder in his back pocket. "Here's the email address for you to email the video. Do that first and we'll work on the paperwork until you come in, then we'll add your statements."

"Thank you. How much longer until my car is cleared?"

"Likely a couple of hours."

Josh took a deep breath. Pulling his phone out of his pocket, he dialed Diego.

"Hey bro, I need a favor. I need a new rental car. Can you guys pick Isabella and me up at the hospital on Fourteenth Avenue? I'll drop you at a rental car agency and you can pick up a new rental. I've got to get back to Nuevo

Laredo. Mateo has less than three hours before fingers start coming off."

"Shit. We'll be right there."

He pulled Isabella to a waiting area a short distance away where they could watch out the windows and he emailed the video to the police station. Just as that was sent, two more police cars sped up to the entrance and two officers ran into the building and made their way through the crowd, yelling, "Emergency" and "Clear the area please."

They jumped on an elevator and Josh let out a long breath. That was not good.

He took Isabella's hand in his. "Do you know any place in Nuevo Laredo that has a Plástico factory or what that might mean? Is there a different Spanish word that means plastic that I'm not familiar with? Some old folk lore about something happening with plastic? Anything?"

Isabella pulled up her phone and started searching for something. While her fingers danced along her phone screen she said.

"My father is involved on the fringe of a plastics company just outside of La Quemada. I'll ask him if they have any ties in Nuevo Laredo."

She listened as her phone connected and Josh watched the crowd and the bomb squad and for Diego, Travis and/or Shep to come and get them.

"Papa." As Isabella chatted with her father the elevator doors opened and he saw one of the police officers who'd gone up before step off pushing a handcuffed Dominic Juarez in a wheelchair.

As he walked through the crowd, the officer shouted for people to move out of the way, Dominic came into clear view; he was also in ankle chains. His eyes landed on

Josh and a smirk appeared on Dominic's face. Josh's stomach rolled as the reality of what just happened hit him hard. He stood and watched as the officer put Dominic into the back of a squad car.

Isabella stood next to him, her hand found his and she grabbed hold. "Did he…"

"I believe so."

"What about the police officers that were up there guarding them?"

Josh shrugged. "One of them could have been on the take."

"Oh my God." Her voice trailed off as they watched the squad car pull away.

Josh then noticed the back of the car. It wasn't a police cruiser. The license plates were regular plates; the car, painted to match the others, looked official enough, except no numbers on the car signified its number in the fleet lineup, and the spelling across the trunk of Escondido was incorrect and spelled Escondito. Dominic just got away.

33

She was still talking to her father but Josh's posture spoke danger. Urgency. High Alert.

He stood. "We've got to go Isi."

"Papa, let me call you back."

She stood and Josh immediately grabbed her hand pulling her through the crowd and beyond it down a long corridor.

"Isi, don't say anything, just keep walking."

Picking up her pace, she clung to her phone and her handbag with her right hand as her left was held by Josh, and he rushed them through the hospital. Most of the corridors were empty, once or twice they met a nurse or a doctor along the way and he always stepped between them and her.

They seemed to be going to the complete opposite side of the hospital and the further they wove through the large building, the more her anxiety ramped up.

Finally close to the back there was a large windowed room with a few people sitting inside. It appeared to be a family waiting room. Televisions were on, and most of the people inside were looking at their phones.

Pulling them to the wall opposite the room, he stood with his body turned to the side in front of her, looking down the hallway they'd just come from. He pulled his phone from his pocket and pushed a couple of buttons.

"Diego, where are you?"

She watched him as he spoke. He still seemed as calm as could be, yet his body was rigid, his jaw tight.

"Okay. Come to the back of the hospital by the..." He looked around for a sign. "The orthopedic entrance. Text me when you get here."

He pocketed his phone and turned to face her.

"The cop taking Dominic from the hospital was not a real cop. Phony cop car. Dominic's now in the wind and we're likely marked. I'm sure he knows what Carlos told us."

She swallowed and processed what he was telling her.

"How did you know? How do you know?"

"Escondido was spelled wrong for one thing. Regular plates. Little things."

"Shit."

"Yeah."

"Will they kill Mateo?"

He gripped both of her shoulders. "Look Isi, I don't know. He's really gotten himself in some deep shit here."

His phone buzzed in his pocket and he pulled it out and saw a text. Dropping it inside his pocket once again he kissed her lips briefly then took her hand and pulled her down the hallway to a door. That door led to a back entrance for orthopedic patients and a reception area. Walking them to the door, he picked up speed once they were outside and opened the back passenger door of

Travis' car, tucking her in the middle of the backseat next to Diego then he climbed in beside her. Travis and Shep were in the front seat and no one said a word.

Josh broke the silence. "Need a rental car. Closest place."

Travis took off, Shep tapped the GPS a couple of times and they drove through the parking lot and then out onto the main road.

Diego finally spoke. "What the fuck is going on?"

Josh filled them in while she sat quietly. Mostly because she was afraid she'd start crying. She'd never been in anything like this before. Nothing. She wasn't sure it was a great idea to come along, but then the thought of being at the house unprotected scared her more and for a half a second she wondered if she should go home with her parents where they were being protected. But then she realized that not knowing what was happening to Josh would be worse than being scared. Closing her eyes to catch up with her feelings on that sobering thought she realized that in such a short amount of time, she'd fallen for this man with his cloak and dagger lifestyle, his dangerous job but his bigger heart. And what was she supposed to do now?

Josh pulled his phone from his pocket.

"Masters."

He listened and she could only hear enough to know it was Gaige on the other end of the line; she tried calculating how long they'd been in the hospital and how much time Mateo had left.

"Can you compare those deposits with title searches at the DOT?"

Listening once more he replied, "Okay," then pocketed his phone again.

Travis pulled into the lot at a rental agency and turned to Josh. "We'll see you back at the house. Stay safe man."

Travis and Shep got out of the car and Diego sat. "I'm coming with you."

"Diego, I'm..."

"Don't man. Just don't. For the first time in ages, and I mean ages, years, I feel like I know what I'm supposed to do. Let me help you. I won't freeze up again. I won't."

Josh jumped from the back of the car, held his hand out to her and just that touch, that firm grip as he pulled her from the car, was electric.

Opening the passenger door, he helped her inside, then darted around the front of the car with a wave to Travis and Shep, who stood at the door to the rental agency watching.

She smiled at them as they pulled away. "You have good friends."

"The best. We all served in the military together. It's a bond that never breaks."

His eyes darted to the mirror and she saw him look back at Diego.

"I get that."

She turned to Diego then. "If you need me to help you in any way to fill out the application for the retraining and therapy program, please let me help you."

Diego swallowed and she could tell he was touched. He nodded slightly. "Thank you."

She smiled at him and hoped he could find what he needed. He'd proven his mettle saving her. Never mind the hesitation. Any person not used to that type of activity, caught off-guard, would have frozen.

Josh then said, "Get ready at the border. We've got to pray for fast."

34

Navigating the lanes of traffic, he maneuvered them to the one that seemed to be going the fastest. That could change of course, but hopefully it wouldn't today. It had already been close to an hour since he'd spoken to Hawk. Mateo now had two hours left.

"Okay. Here we go."

Rolling the window down on the driver's side, the officer stooped at the window.

"Where are you going?"

"Nuevo Laredo."

"What's your purpose?"

"We're going to visit her brother." Josh pointed to Isabella and the officer ducked down to look at her through the driver's side window.

"How long are you staying?"

"Just an hour or two."

Seemingly bored with his constant questions the officer nodded. Pointing to the electronic arm stopping traffic he pushed a button and the arm rose.

Josh eased the car through the opening and slowly merged onto traffic before letting out a deep breath.

"Whew. God is on Mateo's side today. Hopefully."

He didn't look over at Isi, she was worried enough as it was. He adjusted his mirror then checked the GPS for direction. Easing them into the right lane, he settled in for the 20-minute ride.

His phone rang and he quickly answered it on speaker.

"Masters."

"Gaige here. So we've cross checked the bank accounts with titles at the DOT. They match up. What we've figured out is that Mateo bought cars. A lot of them. In the past two years it appears he purchased more than fifty cars. All from various sources. In most cases, those titles were then transferred to other owners. The owners all appear to be from outside the U.S. But, there's no information on shipping the vehicles across the border. I think your hunch is correct in that he's a straw-buyer."

Josh nodded. "So, he has a partner, Dominic Juarez. Dominic is the man who tried to kidnap Isi. I just watched him get into a fake cop car at the hospital. I also suspect before getting sprung, he killed Carlos Mendoza. Anyway can you check that out? We're now on our way back to Nuevo Laredo to meet up with Hawk and Falcon to find Mateo."

"We'll check. Did you get any further information on the plastic building or what that cryptic message might be?"

Josh looked over at Isabella. "Did your father have any information on that front Isi?"

She nodded. "My father, about a year ago, invested in a company located outside of La Quemada. They manufacture plastic bottles and containers for food and beverage companies. The reason he invested is because they were branching out to start up a smaller manufacturing division that produces the plastic bottles used for prescription drugs and pill boxes. That branch of the company converted an older facility just on the outskirts of Nuevo Laredo. He said they always called it the Plastico Edificio. The plastic building in English."

Typing could be heard on the phone and Josh knew Gaige or maybe someone else was searching as they were talking. Then he heard a female voice, which sounded like his sister, Jax, give Gaige an address.

"I'll text you the address. I'll broadcast it to Hawk and Falcon too."

"Is that Jax working with you?"

Jax came on the line. "Yes it's me and you better watch your ass, Brother. Serious as shit here. Keep your head down."

He laughed at her tone. "Shouldn't you be with the twins?"

"Mamá is with them and I needed a break. Plus, my stupid brother got himself caught up in some bullshit and I'm not there to make sure he's safe. AND, if that isn't enough, my husband took a mission this morning. I'm feeling a bit out of sync here."

"Okay. Okay. Settle down Jax. I get it. We'll be fine here."

"Fine? Fine isn't great Josh. Fine is just meh."

He glanced at Isi, and the smile on her face was stunning. She whispered, "Fierce."

All he could do was nod his head.

Jax then said, more to Gaige than him, "Oh, now here's something. It appears that Mateo Martinez has his name on manifestos shipping the plastics products to the U.S."

Josh nodded. It was beginning to come together in his mind now. "Oh, so, here's what I'm piecing together from this side." Josh made a left turn then continued. "Dominic was buying the cars in the U.S. If he's a straw-buyer, he'd need a way to ship the cars over the border. Mateo was responsible for shipping the plastics into the U.S. via shipping containers. He'd tell Dominic where and when the containers would be arriving and Dominic would get the purchased cars to the containers to have them shipped to Mexico where they would be sold, avoiding the taxes and tariffs."

Jax then responded. "Let me call you back. I think that's plausible. I'll see if we can connect the shipping dates from the plastics shipments and the car purchases."

"But, Jax, then where do guns come in? That's what the caller said. He thinks Mateo has his guns."

Josh looked at Isabella. He could see her wheels turning. She then turned to him. "What if Dominic was putting guns in the cars before shipping them to Mexico?"

"So, then what happened to the guns if the man on the phone, who Carlos said was named Tony, didn't get them?"

Isabella turned to him. "Maybe Dominic didn't actually put the guns in a few cars, shorting this Tony. But Tony thinks Mateo took them first."

Seeing the sign for Nuevo Laredo up ahead he told Jax. "Is Gaige still there?"

"Yes, he's on the computers."

"Okay. We're entering Neuvo Laredo. I'm going to hang up so I can get the text to the plastic building. I don't have my comm unit with me so we're flying without."

"Hawk and Falcon have theirs. Stay safe, Brother."

He turned into the town of Neuvo Laredo. "Isi can you get the address up on my GPS?"

Looking at Diego in the back seat what he saw was his friend with a smile on his face."

"What are you smiling at Diego?"

"I feel alive."

35

Isabella pulled up the directions on Josh's phone and watched for the road signs. Her mind reeled with all that Mateo had gotten involved in this time. They only had an hour and twenty minutes before Mateo began losing fingers.

"Isi, put the address to the factory on your phone and use mine to dial Hawk or Falcon."

She found Hawk's number and tapped it, listening as it began to ring. She then put it on speaker.

"Hawk."

Josh spoke quickly. "We're here and three miles from the factory. Where are you?"

"We're across the street from the factory. It's open today and there are employees coming and going. Unless they have sworn everyone to secrecy, which I doubt would work, they either have a secret entrance, or are holding Mateo somewhere else."

"Okay. When we get there, we'll split up and see what we can find. Hang tight."

Josh made a right turn into a parking lot one street over and put the car in park.

"Do you see that?" he asked.

She peered in the direction Josh indicated. "It's a shipping and receiving lot."

"Right. What if they have Mateo in a shipping container?"

Diego sat forward. "That would keep him out of sight and, locked in a container, he'd be secure."

Josh looked at her, then his phone. Taking it from her hand he looked at the time on it. "Employees are likely off work in about a half hour. That leaves time for stragglers filtering out and them to get to Mateo. Likely why they chose this time."

Her eyes scanned the yard for anything that looked like a human could be inside. Of course she couldn't see anything different from one container to another and they were a distance away.

Josh twisted in his seat and looked at her. "Isi. I need you to stay here in the car. I'll bring it closer to that shipping yard over there, but then you need to stay here, in the driver's seat and be ready if we come running. Can you do that?"

"Of course." Her heartbeat sped up and she second-guessed her adamant protest to be part of this adventure or mission or whatever Josh would call it.

Josh put the car in gear and maneuvered them through the parking lot, finding a space about three rows from the edge of the lot and pointed the car in a forward-facing direction.

"Keep your phone on and handy in case we call and if anyone approaches the car, do not get out. Only crack the window open, not all the way in case someone would reach in and if they stick a gun in your face, step on the gas and get the fuck out of here. Got it?"

"Yes."

"That also means keep the car in gear and your foot on the brake."

"Yes."

"Diego, ready?"

"Yeah, I'm ready."

Josh leaned forward and kissed her lips. "Be careful Isi."

"I'm sitting in the car. You be careful."

Josh unbuckled his seat belt and stepped from the car. Isi opened her door and walked around to the driver's side. Josh rewarded her with another kiss on the lips, this one soft and sweet. He looked deep into her eyes. "I've fallen in love with you, Isabella Martinez."

Her mind reeled with that information but before she could say anything he nudged her into the driver's seat and closed the door. Diego climbed out of the backseat and the two together walked to the back of the parking lot away from the car. She watched them, Josh offering suggestions to Diego and as they neared the rear of the parking lot he lifted his phone to his ear.

Soon, they both looked around. Diego pulled his phone from his pocket and soon they both split into different directions and disappeared amid the various shipping containers in the next parking lot.

She cracked the window to see if she could hear anything and occasionally she looked around to make sure someone wasn't watching her. Then she had the thought that she shouldn't watch in the direction Josh and

Diego had gone because if someone was watching her, they'd see her looking that way.

Swallowing she muttered. "There's so much to consider in this line of work."

If she knew nothing else, she knew she'd made the right decision in becoming a doctor; she liked the stability of going to work and not having to look over her shoulder all the time.

A sadness floated over her then at the thought of going back to her job at the clinic in Magnolia; though she loved it there, Josh wouldn't be there. He said he loved her. He'd fallen in love with her. It had only been a few short days and so much had happened in those few days. They hadn't even had a real date. Or courtship. Or more than an hour or so of alone-time at the hotel.

She squirmed in the seat as she remembered having sex with Josh. His body fit hers so well. The way his hands felt on her body was imprinted forever. Her father had proposed to her mother on their second date. It happened that fast and it has been a lasting relationship. Strong.

Did she love Josh?

A gun shot rang out and she instantly scanned the area it sounded from, seeing two men run from the back of the building toward the area Josh and Diego had disappeared in. Her heart raced and she made sure she had the car in gear as she continued to scan the area.

"Where are you?"

Another shot sounded and she saw one of the men run between two containers. He disappeared and reappeared at the other end of the container. Looking for the second man, she couldn't see him and her eyes scanned feverishly for Josh and Diego.

It hurt to breathe as she waited to see what happened.

She'd never be able to get over there in time with the car and was doubtful the car would fit between the containers. As she scanned the area once more a tap sounded from the back driver's-side window; reflected in the mirror, a man stood alongside the car, a gun pointed at her head.

36

Josh ran as the gunman shot between the containers at him. He was still too far away to hit him, dumbass. He'd given up his position with the first shots. Gun up, Josh listened for footsteps. In the silence a faint pounding on metal could be heard. He listened for the sound again, and inched toward it. Another shot rang out and he flattened himself against a container, listening for both footsteps and the tapping.

Gravel under someone's feet crunched, and he followed that sound over two containers. Peering around one of them, he saw the gunman two containers up from where he was. Another shot rang out and hit the side of the container Josh stood behind and he knew he needed to move.

Diego yelled, "Hey, asshole."

Feet crunching then more shots and he quickly peered around and saw the gunman running down the aisle away from his position and to the left. Diego was baiting them. Josh moved as quietly as he could and heard the tapping once more.

"Stupid fucker." Diego baited again and Josh ran down the long side of the red metal unit to one more row back. The space between them was slight, but enough a person could walk through without turning to the side. The echo between the containers amplified his breathing as it reverberated through the tunnel created by these large storage vessels.

The faint sound of the pounding could be heard closer this time. Noting it came from alongside him, he ducked and ran to the back of the blue receptacle with the bold white letters ENOS, he had heard the tapping from inside and listened again.

Tap. Tap. Tap.

There was a ladder at the back of the container and Josh slowly climbed up on top of the ladder and lay on his belly on the top. Sliding down to the far end, he could see several rows at a time and found Diego running behind the large metal boxes and yelling at the gunmen.

"Dumb as fucking rocks." Diego yelled again, then took off running. Seeing one of the gunmen in his sights, he aimed and shot, hitting him in the arm, which didn't stop him, only slowed him down. Josh ducked, his location compromised. Then he saw Hawk and Falcon from the far side of the yard. They entered behind containers and he saw them separate, Hawk to the left, Falcon to the right.

That's when his heart stopped in his chest. A gunman standing next to the car with a gun pointed at Isi. He'd never be able to hit him from here and not put her in danger. Checking around for the gunmen, he noted both of them were now walking to the left toward Hawk and Diego. Scrambling down the front of the container, he took off running toward Isi, his heart wrestling to catch up with the thrumming in his ears so loud he couldn't hear anything else. A shot rang out and hit a container just behind him and he dropped to the ground. Scooting alongside a container, he waited, peeked out and saw a gunman running toward him. Josh raised his gun, saw Falcon coming up the aisle in front of him and dropped his aim; he gestured to Falcon, showing him the direction of the gunman and Falcon nodded.

Josh then took off running up the side of the container and made a sharp left toward the parking lot. Another shot rang out and he heard a thud, hoping it was the gunman and not Falcon. The man alongside the car took a step toward the containers at the sound of that shot. Another shot rang out, dropping him to the ground alongside the car.

Isi punched the gas, driving toward him at the yard. Two more shots and his phone rang.

"Both men are down."

"Diego and Falcon?"

"I'm looking at Diego."

Hawk's comm unit then clicked. "Falcon alive."

Huffing out air he asked, "Are there more men coming out?"

"I don't see any. Falcon and I are going inside to see if we can find Tony Morales."

"Roger. I think I heard Mateo tapping in one of the containers, I'll see if I can find it."

"Roger. Hawk out."

He ended the call and peered over at Isi. Holding his hand up, he silently asked her to wait and he climbed down the outside ladder to the ground. He ran to her.

"Are you all right?" he yelled as he neared.

She jumped from the car and ran to him. They met

and her arms wrapped around his neck and pulled him close. He could feel her body shaking against him and he pulled her close to him and squeezed her tightly.

"It's okay baby. It's okay."

Her heavy breathing in his neck spoke volumes to the fact that she was way out of her element here. Dread filled his stomach at the thought that she wouldn't be able to handle him going out on missions—what would they do moving forward?

Feeling her calm slightly, he said, "I think I know where Mateo is. Can you follow me in the car? It'll fit down the horizontal aisles."

She swallowed and he saw tears in her eyes. "Yes, I can do that."

"Okay. Hey, it's okay. We're all okay."

"Not all of us."

"All of us are fine. Those men, would have killed us if we hadn't killed them first and remember, they have been holding your brother hostage for the better part of three days now."

She peered deeply into his eyes and he swiped away the tears from under hers.

"I love you too."

"Don't feel obligated to..."

"No. I don't. I love you Josh Masters."

His heart—man, the commotion it was creating inside his body right now was a sensation he'd never felt before.

He kissed her quickly. "More of that later."

"Definitely."

He briskly walked her to the car and set her inside the driver's side seat. "Follow me."

She put the car in gear and slowly inched the car forward behind him as he listened for the tapping. He tapped on each container listening for a return sound. On the fourth container he heard it. He tapped again and got a response.

There was a chain on the container and he walked back to the car. "Isi, I need something to open this with. Do you have a paperclip, hair thingy, wire or something?"

37

Isabella dug through her purse and found a couple of bobby pins. She handed them to Josh, who immediately stretched one open all the way and the other one he shoved into the bottom of the lock. He worked the lock, pushing then pulling the bobby pins from under the lock and it opened up.

Diego came running and Josh turned and looked at her. Holding his hand up asking her to stay in the car she nodded, but she wanted to run in there and see if Mateo was inside. She didn't have her medical bag with her and her parents' house was at least a 45-minute drive, depending on the medical care he'd need.

Josh and Diego disappeared into the container and she heard more gun shots from inside the building they were behind. She jumped at the sounds but stayed where she was. Checking that the doors were locked, she watched the opening to the container barely able to breathe. It seemed to be taking them an awfully long time and her fears that Mateo was already dead started to roll through her mind. He may have been dead all this time for all they knew.

"Come on Josh." she whispered.

More gun shots sounded and her heart rate ratcheted up tenfold. Those sounded closer than the last ones. Isabella glanced up into the rearview mirror. She didn't see anyone, which made her feel mildly better. But as soon as she looked forward again, there stood Dominic directly in front of her with a gun pointed at her.

In a split second she dropped down across the console and hit the gas, sending the car flying forward as gun shots rained in through the windshield. Shards of glass rained down on her before she felt the thud and then the crash of the car hitting something solid.

"Isi!" She heard Josh's panicked voice scream her name. "Isi?"

The driver's door was roughly pulled open and hands began pulling her out of the car.

"Isi. Talk to me."

She could hear him talking to her but it felt like she was submerged under water. Josh slid his hand under her legs while he reached in and pulled her up by grabbing hold of her sweater. His arm then circled her back and pulled her from the vehicle.

The fresh air helped to bring her around and the sounds began to come back to her. He set her on the trunk of the car and looked into her eyes.

"Are you hit?"

He examined her head, her neck, her torso. Weakly she said, "No. I don't think so."

"Oh my God, Isi. You scared the shit out of me."

"I'm fine. I..." She blinked, "Oh my God, did I kill him?"

She tried to turn her head but Josh held her in place. "Don't look."

"Oh my God. I did, didn't I?"

Tears streamed from her eyes as she realized that she'd broken the Hippocratic oath, "first do no harm."

Josh held her in his arms and she could hear activity going on around her but she felt lost in her anguish, she'd done what no doctor should do.

"Isi." A weak voice from her right side called to her.

She turned and saw a very dirty, sweaty Mateo leaning against the back of the car.

She gasped and grabbed Mateo and hugged him. "Matty. I'm so relieved you're still alive."

"Me too."

His voice was weak and he smelled awful. She pulled back and looked at him. He had cuts and bruises where he'd clearly been beaten. He didn't stand tall, he was slightly hunched forward.

She jumped from the back of the car and immediately went into doctor mode. She checked for all ten fingers, then looked into his eyes and noticed his pupils were constricted, but they were outside and it was sunny, so that was to be expected. He wore what used to be a white button up shirt but which now was smeared with blood and grime. Unbuttoning his shirt, she looked at his torso, and noticed large bruising. Touching a spot on his ribs that protruded, he gasped and she assessed that he had, if not a broken rib, a cracked rib. But, likely broken.

"Josh, we have to get him to the hospital."

"No." Mateo yelled, as much as he could anyway. He winced as he said it and shook his head no. "He has reach."

"Who has reach? Tony?"

Mateo only nodded.

Josh then asked, "Do you only have the one car still at home?"

"Yes."

They were a few blocks from Mateo's house and besides, Tony, or someone, had access to Mateo's house at the moment. They couldn't very well drive this car through the city with a shot up windshield. He was having a tough time with cars this week.

Hawk and Falcon walked from between the containers and stood with their backs to them in a guarding stance.

Diego walked to the front of the car and she turned to see that she'd pinned Dominic to the side of a container. He lay across the top of the car, blood dripping from his mouth and running in a stream across the hood and down the side.

"Don't look Isi." Josh got into her line of vision and stared into her eyes. His head shook but he never looked away.

Diego dug in Dominic's pockets and found keys. Walking toward the parking area for employees of the factory he began pressing the fob until a car unlocked and a horn honked. He turned to them, "We have a car."

"That's stealing," she immediately responded.

"I don't think he's going to need it and we do." Diego responded.

What on earth had she gotten herself into? Here she'd been condemning Mateo for getting involved in something he shouldn't and in the matter of a few hours she'd almost been kidnapped, shot and then she'd killed someone. Now she was stealing a car.

Diego walked to the parking lot and got into Dominic's car. Police sirens sounded and Hawk turned around.

"Gaige is on it. Since this involved arms and transport across country borders, Casper may get involved which will help tremendously."

"Mateo, you need medical attention."

"Not from a hospital. Take me to Mamá and Papas. You are my doctor."

Josh looked over at Hawk, "Bud, what about Tony?"

"No Tony. But we got a lead on him and Casper is likely going to look into him. He's Cuban."

"Matty, what on earth did you do?" She was fearful for what was yet to come.

"Isi, I didn't do anything. Dominic..." Mateo looked over at Dominic laying across the hood of the car "Dominic was packing our cars with weapons. He stole from Tony but pinned it on me."

Diego pulled up in Dominic's SUV and opened the back driver's side door. He approached Mateo, "Let me get you inside bud."

"It's not stealing Isi, it's my car. One I bought and had shipped here."

Mateo put an arm around Diego's shoulders and as gently as he could, Diego slowly walked him over to the car.

She watched for some time, then looked at Josh, "I don't even recognize myself today."

He swiped at the moisture left on her face and kissed the tip of her nose.

"I recognize you. You're the woman I love."

38

Josh took Isi's hand and walked to Hawk. "What's next?"

"Gaige is on the phone right now with local police and Casper at the same time."

"What about us? Do you need us to stay?"

"Gaige says go and take care of Mateo. They'll give police the Martinez address and they'll likely come out for statements."

Josh hesitated and Hawk smirked. "Things run differently here bro. Go on."

Josh fist bumped Hawk, nodded to Falcon and walked Isabella to Dominic's or Mateo's car. He'd get the full story once Mateo was in better condition to talk.

Arriving at the SUV, Isi got into the passenger back seat next to Mateo and started taking vitals. He climbed in the front passenger seat; Diego took the driver's position.

"Do you need the GPS to get us back to La Quemada?"

"No. I've got it."

Diego drove them from the parking lot and out to the

road. Once they were on the highway Josh nudged Diego. "You did good man."

Diego smiled. "Thanks. It all kind of comes back to you. The training stuff I mean."

"Yeah, it does." He watched the road for a while. "What about the other stuff? The PTSD?"

Diego frowned. "I'll let you know in a couple of days. Sometimes it comes at night or during weird times."

Josh listened to Isabella talk to Mateo and ask him questions. She was a good doctor. She managed to set her personal comments aside as she assessed Mateo's condition.

"Tell me what happened Mateo, so I know the best direction for assessment."

"Carlos picked me up at the bachelor party. Late, close to midnight I guess."

He struggled to breathe, his words came in spurts. "Carlos had told me the day before that Tony was pissed and that he had things missing. I thought he meant a car or two were missing. I told him all cars had been shipped. Dominic took care of getting the vehicles in the containers and sending me the packing slips and then sending me the original manifest by email."

He squirmed as she touched sore spots on his chest. "He had to then doctor the manifest for customs."

Isabella shook her head but continued to listen.

"I told him I'd get them the manifests to show him. He didn't believe me. Said I was stupid."

Isi took a deep breath. "Is that how you got the black-eye?"

Mateo nodded and Isi gently felt around his eye socket, which was now beginning to turn green, for broken bones.

"The night of the wedding he picked me up and I had more manifests for him. That's when he told me he wanted the guns. Two of his goons worked me over. They had me tied to a pole in another building. Then today or yesterday or sometime, they tossed me in the shipping container. He said he'd start cutting my fingers off in twenty-four hours if I didn't tell them where the guns were."

"Dominic laughed and looked me in the eye and said, 'Man, you've got to give him his guns back.'" Mateo swallowed. "I knew what he'd done then."

Josh turned and looked at Mateo. "We need Dominic's U.S. address and anything else you can tell us to tie him to the missing guns."

Mateo nodded. "I have it at home. Top desk drawer."

Josh shook his head. "I doubt it's still there, bud. They've been inside your place. They left your phone there for us to find."

Mateo was quiet for a while. "I have another place. At the office at Martinez Agua."

"Once we get you situated at home, we'll check it out."

Josh pulled out his phone and called Hawk.

"Yeah."

"Dominic was packing the cars with weapons. Tony is the buyer. Mateo has information on Dominic as to where he lived in the U.S., his places of business, etc. We might be able to find the missing guns or evidence of them there to tie him to the weapons. Also, Mateo says there are two copies of the manifests proving the straw operation. If all Mateo gets is pinched on the straw operation, he may be able to avoid prison with a hefty fine. After all, the main crime is nonpayment of tariffs and taxes."

"On it. Send me those addresses as soon as you can.

Once we're finished here, Falcon and I will go see what we can find."

"Roger. Out."

Sitting straight ahead he mulled over all they'd just learned. It would be impossible to get Tony if he went back to Cuba.

Twisting in his seat to look at Mateo. "How does Tony fly here?"

"Private."

Nodding he asked, "Do you know which airport?"

"Yeah." Mateo paused to catch his breath.

Isabella spoke for him. "It's Air Quemada."

Josh turned to face forward. Tapping Gaige's number he held his phone to his ear.

"Whatcha got?"

Josh chuckled. "There's a private airport just outside of La Quemada named Air Quemada. This Tony flies in there on a private plane. He's Cuban, so he'll be hard to catch if he leaves here."

"Okay. I'm on it. Great job with the intel and the rescue. How's Mateo doing?"

"He'll be fine, he's pretty beat up though."

"Yeah, figures. Better than dead. Out."

Josh lowered his phone and stared out the window. There were a lot of balls in the air but they were getting closer. If they could find information on the straw operation and the guns in Dominic's house or office, locate Tony before he left the country and not have to serve time in Mexico for the men they'd killed, this could all get wrapped up in time for Travis' wedding. The whole reason he was here in the first place. He felt like he'd been here for a year, so much had happened.

Diego turned them into La Quemada and Josh breathed a sigh of relief. At least they'd get Mateo some help and he could hydrate and eat.

Diego looked up ahead and said, "Uh oh."

39

A roadblock up ahead. Mateo looked up and winced, each and every bump in the road gave him great pain and now, he'd likely have to step out of the car and get back in which was going to give him even more discomfort. The mad sister in her decided he'd created this mess and deserved it, but the doctor in her wanted to alleviate his pain as much as she could.

Pulling her medical ID from her purse, she got it ready and hoped it would get them somewhere in not disturbing her patient, which is what Mateo was to her now.

Josh got on his phone. "Gaige, we're running into a roadblock driving into La Quemada. Do you know if they're looking for us?"

She listened as Diego slowed the car behind the other cars waiting to get through. She looked as far as she could up ahead and saw that no one was being asked to leave their vehicles, so hopefully it was simply a random check point. And horrible timing at that.

"Thanks." Josh ended his call. "They're not looking for us."

Their car slowly inched along the road until they got to the officers conducting the roadblock. The officer leaned down and looked at them all, then blanched when he saw Mateo.

"You need a doctor sir?"

Mateo pointed at her with his thumb. "She's my doctor. I'm trying to get home for treatment."

His breathing came in two-to-three-word spurts. For good measure, Isabella held up her medical ID and the officer looked at it, then her. He stared for a while and Josh broke the stare down.

"What are you looking for, Officer?"

"Nothing. It's routine. If you can show us the registration we'll be all set."

Josh opened the glove box and pulled out some paperwork. Sifting through it he handed a copy of the title to the officer. The title was still in Mateo's name as it hadn't been sold yet.

The officer looked in at Josh, "You Mateo Martinez?"

"No sir, he is." He pointed with his thumb to the backseat.

The officer's eyes darted to the backseat at the same time Mateo tried to shift his position and cried out as pain shot through him.

Isabella tried to comfort him, and the officer must have decided it wasn't worth it to question further. He handed the title to Diego from the driver's side window and nodded.

"You may pass through."

Diego handed Josh the title and Mateo let out a very

shallow relieved sigh. Isabella looked at him. "Were you worried?"

"Of course. I have no idea what else Carlos has been up to. To check the registration never occurred to me."

She then let out a sigh of relief and hoped they'd be able to make it to her parents without further incident. Pulling her phone from her purse, she dialed her father.

"Hi Papa. We have Mateo. We're on our way to your house. He's been badly beaten and needs medical care, but is afraid to go to the hospital. I just wanted to let you know so Jonny is aware we'll be approaching. We're driving a..."

She looked around and Josh turned to her. "A 2020 Dodge Durango. White."

"Josh is with you?"

"Yes and Diego. Just the four of us."

"Okay Isi, we'll be ready for you."

"Thank you Papa. Is everything all right there?"

"Yes, it's been quiet here."

"Okay. Good. See you in fifteen minutes. Love you."

"I love you too Isi."

The line went dead and she breathed out a sigh of relief.

The drive continued, quietly. Another fifteen minutes into the drive Diego once again said, "Oh no."

Isabella looked up and her parents driveway was blocked and guarded. "That's just Johnny's people. It'll be fine."

Diego rolled the window down as they approached and Isabella dialed her father's phone. After four rings the phone stopped ringing and he didn't answer. Her brows furrowed and she tried once again but received the same results.

She then looked up her mother's phone number and clicked "call".

Her mother's phone rang only twice before her mom answered her phone.

"Isi are you here?"

"Yes Mamá. I see the driveway is blocked. Can you let them know it's us and to let us in?"

"Of course. Just give me a minute."

The line went dead and she watched the guards receive a phone call and then open the barricade to let them pass through. They looked into the car as they drove past them. She sighed again, hoping the weird uncomfortable feelings would end soon.

Mateo turned his head to look at her. "I'm sorry Isi. I never meant for any of this to happen."

She softened up but just a bit. "I know Matty. But, you've just got to stop this illegal activity. You continue to bring Mamá and Papa and the rest of us down with your shenanigans."

She turned to look into his eyes, which was hard. His left eye was yellowed from the punch he'd taken. It was also swollen and discolored around it. Certainly not her handsome brother from days before.

"I know Isi. I know." He looked forward as Diego slowly stopped alongside the sidewalk to the front door. He opened his door, unbuckled his seat belt and got out of the car at the same time as Josh. Opening her door, Josh held his hand out to her and she gladly took it. The instant they touched, the wrongs of the world seemed right. At least until she heard Mateo groan and then cry out as pains shot through him again.

Josh stared into her eyes. He leaned forward and

lightly kissed her on the lips then whispered. "Let's get him inside."

"Thank you Josh. For everything."

His smile rivaled the sun and she thought he was the most handsome man she'd ever seen. She also realized that despite a few cuts and scrapes along his face and neck, which she looked closer at now, after all they'd been through, he looked remarkably unscathed.

She touched one of his cuts and he smiled. "I'm fine. He needs your help. And you may need some assistance with those tiny cuts on your face from the windshield."

She touched her face and felt the dried blood in several spots. Josh's smile grew again. "I'm happy to play doctor with you later and take care of you."

A voice clearing from the opposite side of the car had them both turning their heads to see her father watching them.

It took them a while to get Mateo into the house. It was a slow process for him but they had no other way to get him inside without it hurting. A stretcher would have helped, but nothing of the sort was available. Finally getting him to his room, Josh helped Isi gather items she needed, then helped undress Mateo. Which he now reminded himself, was the second Martinez brother he'd gotten undressed. But at least he didn't have to haul Mateo to the shower. He left Isi and Mateo alone so she could help him and assess what he needed until they could convince him to go to the hospital.

He walked up the steps to the area of the house between the living room and the kitchen.

Bianca and Ivan sat in the living room with Diego chatting and he joined them. Just as he sat his phone rang and he saw Gaige's name on the screen. He looked at both of the Martinez's and said, "Excuse me please."

He stood and left. He answered the call as he walked from the living room to the kitchen.

"Masters."

"Okay, so here's what we've managed. Mexican police were trying to figure out who was behind some of the arms-smuggling going on and they are happy with our involvement. Not with all the dead bodies, but they're happy to at least have this much. They need the information on Carlos. Have you gathered that intel yet?"

"No, I was just about to ask Mr. Martinez to come with me to the office and see what we can find."

"Okay. You do that. Hawk and Falcon are finishing up with the police and they'll head back to the U.S. and wait for intel on Carlos' house and office. They'll be at the rental in the meantime."

"Roger. I'll get back to you within the hour. Out."

He hung up his phone and walked back to the living room.

Mr. Martinez stopped talking when he walked in the room and they all looked at him.

"Mr. Martinez."

"Ivan, please."

"Ivan. I need you to come with me to Martinez Agua to check over Mateo's office. We need Carlos Mendoza's United States address for both his home and his office. Mateo says he has it there."

Ivan looked him in the eye and concern was written all over his face. "How much trouble is Matty in this time?"

Josh let out a breath. "I'm not going to lie, I don't know. Right now, he's been operating a straw buying scam, importing cars into Mexico and Cuba, circumventing taxes and tariffs. It's a white-collar crime and the only victims are the governments because of the nonpayment of taxes. But, if we can't get the information on where Carlos was operating from or any information on the guns and where he was buying them or stealing them from and how he was packing them in cars, Mateo could also be implicated in that too. That is going to be much more serious and will involve prison time. And, since the gun buyer is who had Mateo held hostage, I'd say he would likely be able to reach Mateo in prison. So, I hate to be so blunt, but pinning this on Carlos may save Mateo's life."

Bianca softly cried and Ivan's face fell as he then looked at the floor between his feet. He suddenly looked like an old man.

Isabella walked into the room at that moment and ran to her mother. "Mamá, it's going to be all right. I'm sure of it."

He watched her calm her mother, then she turned her gaze toward him. As if a magnetic pull attracted them, she came to him and he immediately held his arm out for her to step into his embrace. He tucked her into his side, his right arm wrapped around her and kissed the top of her head. She wrapped her arms around his waist and the feeling was exhilarating. Her parents now knew.

Ivan looked into his eyes. His eyes then took in Isabella in his embrace, looked into her eyes then he nodded.

"I can see you have been a guardian angel to my family. Let me get my keys and I'll drive you to the office."

Ivan turned to Bianca and she stood and hugged her husband close. They whispered a few words to each other then he kissed his wife's lips and left the room.

Bianca turned toward them, her eyes still watery, but her smile genuine. "I see you have at last stopped fighting the pull between you."

Isi giggled. "Yes. Though, nothing is ever certain."

She looked up at him and he squeezed her again. "There are never guarantees Isi."

Ivan walked from the office and Josh kissed Isi briefly, then reluctantly let her go. Turning to Diego, "Do you want to come with us?"

"Of course."

Diego nodded to Bianca and Isabella and followed Ivan and Josh to the front door. The air outside was humid and the sounds of birds and frogs was loud as the evening neared.

Ivan was first to speak. "The office should be mostly empty this time of the day, which is good. Hopefully it won't raise any suspicions in case there is someone there working with Mateo on this ridiculous operation."

Josh chose to remain silent. What could he say? This poor man had had a lifetime of his kid being bad and was now faced with whether to fix it for him yet again or let him go it alone. Sadly all his fixing it was why they were here right now, but Josh had no children and couldn't actually say what he'd do in the same situation. If Maya or Myles got into trouble, he'd do what he could for them and try to fix it, so no matter, it was always a tough choice.

Then he wondered if Isabella wanted children one day. That thought stopped him in his tracks.

"Anything wrong bro?" Diego asked.

Her mother walked to her and wrapped her in a warm hug. Whispering in her ear, "I'm so happy you have found your love."

"Mamá, it's just new and nice in some respects, but we've been under fire or attack since we've gotten to know each other. What if when the dust settles, it's over? It might be boring."

Her mother laughed out loud then. "Oh querida, I see how he looks at you. If you are bored with that man, there is something wrong with you. The heat is there, always smoldering under the surface, waiting for you."

Her cheeks burned hot as her mother stepped back and looked into her eyes. "Ah yes, it is there for you, too."

"Mamá. Stop."

"You will see when you have daughters and sons of your own, you'll be able to tell when they meet the one. It's always there even when they can't see it. Remember when Eric first met Cecily? He said she was too skinny and too immature and too young. He looked for all the reasons not to be attracted to her. But, when he looked at her and thought no one else was looking, it was there. That burning desire. That love. I saw it."

She remembered giggling about it with Emiliana many times. "Oh Eric, he's such a liar," they joked. They'd giggle and laugh as they watched them from afar. Her cheeks heated again and her legs felt weak.

"If that's true Mamá, and Josh is my true love, what will I do? I wanted to open my own clinic in Magnolia. I've made plans. I've built my practice there. Josh, he will never leave his job. And he shouldn't, he's amazing at it."

"Why does your clinic have to be in Magnolia? Do you think sick people only live in Magnolia? There are likely sick people where he lives too. Open a clinic there."

Isabella sat on the sofa, her mother followed.

"Sometimes querida, when we sacrifice the most for someone we love, we find the biggest reward. My guess is, if you asked Josh to leave his job and find something in Texas like it, he would try. You have to look at some of these things. Is there something comparable in Texas for Josh to do? Is there something in Indiana comparable for you to do? Who would be giving up the most?"

Looking into her mother's eyes she let her mother's wise words set in.

"Well, we aren't anywhere near that decision. It's only been a few days."

"Remember, your father asked me to marry him on our second date. We knew then."

Isabella looked out the window and tried to calm the raging emotions in her heart and in her mind. She'd dreamed of her clinic in Magnolia for years. She'd even started looking at land and had the layout in her clinic settled in her mind. She'd be giving all of that up. Of course she could be a doctor anywhere.

But, it had never occurred to her to give up her dreams for someone else. That likely made her very selfish.

Emiliana walked downstairs and gasped when she saw Isabella on the sofa.

"Oh, Isi, you're home."

Isabella ran to her sister and wrapped her in a mighty hug.

"I'm happy to see you're doing well today. This has been stressful to say the least."

Emi nodded. "I've largely stayed up in my room working. The nice thing about working from a remote site is it can be remote from anywhere." Emi looked into her eyes. "Did you find Matty?"

"Yes, he's downstairs in his room. He's been badly beaten but he's too afraid to go to a hospital. I've done the best I can with what I had here to work with. He needs X-rays. He likely needs more medical attention than I can offer. But, he also needs to rest and I've gotten him some electrolytes and nourishment for now, which will go a long way to help him heal."

Isabella turned to her mother. "Mamá, did Eric and Cecily get on their plane without issue?"

"Yes. He texted a while ago. They are in the air now."

"Okay." Taking Emi's hand she pulled her to the sofa. "Tell me what you've been working on so we can all get our minds off of this nightmare for a while."

"I've been working on a new logo and promotional graphics for Martinez Agua and Martinez Holdings. Papa wanted something more modern."

"That sounds fun."

Her phone chimed a text and she read it. Her heart began beating wildly.

"They found it. They found what they were looking for."

Her mother sobbed and covered her mouth with her hands and Emiliana looked on in confusion.

"Papa went with Josh and Diego to see if they could locate paperwork to tell them where Carlos' home and office in the U.S. were. We need that to clear Matty of gun running crimes."

"Oh my God, are you kidding? Running guns? Over the border?" Emi turned to their mother. "Mamá, you cannot get him out of this this time. He keeps getting in trouble. He'll bring all of us down. Look what's happened to Isi this week. No more. I swear it, if you and Papa get him out of this mess I will move to the U.S. with Isi and I won't come back."

"Emi, we don't want him to go to jail."

"Then you choose him over us. I hope your troubled brat is worth it."

Emi stomped up the stairs and Isi watched her with tears in her eyes. Taking a deep breath she swiped away the tears that spilled with the pads of her fingers. She felt the same way this time. She felt it last time and then got stuck once more, but she was finished.

She walked to the kitchen to get something to drink. Iced tea sounded refreshing. She'd forgotten to ask Josh if he'd be staying here for the night or if they were going back to the rental. Should she even go with him? She was the only woman in a house full of men. Travis, Shep and Diego were trying to celebrate Travis' upcoming wedding, though that had also been marred by her brother. Hawk and Falcon, though not all that talkative, seemed determined to get their work done and head home, so they may not have to be around very long. And then what? She'd go home to Magnolia?

That thought depressed her. She froze as she poured her tea from the beautiful cut glass pitcher into her glass. Swallowing, she set the pitcher on the counter and took a sip of her tea. Her hand shook slightly as her mind scattered in all different directions.

A car pulling into the garage snapped her back to reality.

He snapped pictures of the addresses on the papers. Took the manifests from the drawer and a few files of some of the cars. Titles were still in his possession which meant they weren't sold yet. So, they needed to find these cars. If Tony tried to transport them to Cuba, he'd have to have some means to do that. They likely needed to match up these titles with cars in the parking lot at the plastics factory. Since most of the employees had gone for the day and there were still cars in the lot, it was likely some of the cars were still there. Couple that with the fact that they were being shipped to and from that location. That was something he and Diego could do. Maybe it could wait until first thing in the morning since going tonight would be highly unsafe. But, he did wonder if local law enforcement would watch the parking lot so the cars didn't disappear.

He phoned Gaige and was surprised when Jax answered. "Hey bro, what's up?"

"Jax, what are you doing there? You should be home with the kids."

"You did not just say that to me. Take it back before I hang up."

He huffed out a breath. "I'm sorry. I didn't mean like your place was at home, I just meant it's late and you still need to rest Jax."

"I'm okay and I can't rest because my brother is still in danger." She quieted then continued. "Besides, I want to hear more about Isabella Martinez."

His eyes darted to Ivan Martinez digging through a file cabinet across the room and Diego on the other side of the desk combing through files.

"It'll have to wait. Promise, though. What I need to know is if you have connections with local police and would they watch the lot of the plastics factory tonight to make sure cars aren't stolen or shipped away from there. I'm thinking some of these cars that Mateo and Carlos were shipping might still be in the lot. I have titles here and will need to match them up to vehicles but it's not safe there tonight and difficult in the dark."

He could hear tapping on the keyboard. "I have a contact here, let me give them a call. Are you okay after today's fun and games?"

"Yeah. Nothing but a few scratches and scrapes."

"Okay. I'll get back to you."

The line went dead. Jax was on it and would likely not take any answer but "we'll do it." But, they still had to trust that local police weren't corrupt. He knew nothing about this country or the players within it.

Ivan turned to look at him. "I have some files here I need for the business. We've been losing money recently and I'll need to have accountants come in and find out if Mateo or someone else was skimming. That's my problem. When you have what you need, we should get back home. Elisa will have supper waiting for us."

He looked over at Diego, "How are you doing over there?"

"Good. There's nothing in these drawers that seem to be related to Carlos, cars, shipping or anything but water, packaging, labels, and personnel files."

"Grab the personnel files. Maybe we'll find some names in there we are familiar with. Someone was helping Mateo ship and sell the cars."

Ivan walked from the room and came back a few minutes later with a couple of boxes. "Put your files in here."

They packed up the boxes and walked from Mateo's office and through the empty building. Exiting, he stood to guard Ivan as he locked up, Josh's eyes scanning the area. He was comforted that Diego was doing the same. Their military training did come back to them in situations where it was needed. Diego had been a Godsend during this time, otherwise he'd have been completely on his own.

Placing the boxes in the trunk, they got into Ivan's car and began the fifteen-minute drive back to the Martinez home. Ivan tapped the Bluetooth and a phone began ringing. The dash console read "mi amor."

"Yes dear, is everything all right?"

"Si, si. We are on our way home. Set dinner places for Diego and Josh."

"Of course, we're all ready."

"Home soon."

Without any more words said, dinner was planned out and Josh felt as though they'd be staying the night as well. Which was fine, he needed to be at the plastics factory in the morning to see if they could find the cars. Mateo would hopefully start explaining some of the operation and how they managed it. Then, there was Isabella. Where did they go from here?

"You will be good to her, do you hear me?" Ivan's stern words broke into his thoughts.

Josh blinked. "Of course."

"I mean, if you are not feeling it, you let her go now. She looks at you with love in her eyes. I see it."

Josh swallowed. Turning his head to look at Ivan. "What do I look like when I look at Isi?"

Ivan laughed. "You have that look too. But as her father, it's my place to tell you to be honest with her."

"Noted."

He looked out the windshield once again. The area was beautiful and serene, the birds had tucked in for the night as the dusk settled in and the frogs and grasshoppers began their evening songs. It was still humid but not as hot as it had been during the day.

"Also," Ivan continued.

Josh's stomach twisted a bit. He certainly didn't want to have this conversation. But absolutely not with Diego in the car with them.

"Thank you. Matty has always been our problem child, but this time he's gone too far. I don't know what we would have done without you. And," he looked into the mirror, "you, Diego." He turned on his left turn signal to turn into the driveway. "I think this is just the beginning."

43

She finished setting the table with her mother and thought it was both funny and nerve-racking that her mamá insisted on using the fine china. "We want to make a good impression, Isi."

She stopped and looked her mother in the eye. "We've made quite the impression on Josh, Mamá, but I'm not sure it's a great one. We've been nothing but trouble and he's here to celebrate the marriage of his friend, Travis, whom he's spent only a modicum of time with. We've monopolized his vacation, his friend's wedding, and invaded his personal space more than should be allowed."

Her mother stopped and folded her hands in front of her. She took a deep breath then said, "Well there's nothing that can be done for that now. We'll try to find a way to make it up to him."

"How are you going to do that? He doesn't seem financially motivated at all. He makes great money. He works for a company that is doing very well financially. He travels. He's doing something he loves and he's friggen good at it."

The door opened from the garage and her father walked in with Josh and Diego behind him. All of them carrying boxes.

"We've found many files that we'll need to pour over after dinner."

Her father kissed Mamá as he strode toward his office just past the dining room. Josh, following behind him, winked at her, which did all sorts of crazy things to her body, and a grinning Diego took up the rear.

Her mother went to the kitchen to tell Elisa that they were home and dinner could be served, then checked that everyone had something to drink. Her father liked his tequila but she wasn't sure about Josh and Diego. At the wedding he'd had a couple of beers, but she wasn't sure if that was his drink of choice or not.

He walked back out of the office and walked directly to her. She looked up into his sexy eyes framed with the most envious set of lashes any man should have and smiled at him.

"I'm glad you're back," she whispered.

"Me too." He leaned down and kissed her. "Direct me to the bathroom please, I'd like to wash my hands."

She led him down the hall to the other side of the house between the living room and the kitchen. A small half bath was situated there. She stepped to the side and smiled at him as he faced her, a sweet smile stretched across his kissable lips.

"I'm looking forward to spending some alone time with you Isi. Tomorrow night, plan nothing. We're going out."

"I have to get back to work."

His smile fell. "Play hooky. A few more days. Plus, we

still aren't sure how much of a danger Tony is or where he is. It's not safe for you to go back alone yet."

She studied him—no hardship—then he kissed her. It was a peck at first. Then he kissed her again. This time, their lips completely touched. His were warm and soft, yet slightly commanding. His right hand cupped her jaw, holding her in place; his left arm wrapped around her waist and pulled her into his body. His hard, sexy, warm body. As his tongue dipped into her mouth, certain parts of him grew harder and her body wanted him. All of him.

He nipped at her lips, then whispered, "We've got to get in for dinner, but I want you so badly, Isabella Martinez."

Oh, his deep voice murmuring sexy words like that made her knees weak. "I want you, Josh Masters. Badly."

He chuckled. "Shit, this sucks."

"It does. But, tonight, I'll come to you. I promise."

"Deal."

He nipped her lips once more, then stepped into the bathroom and she took a moment to gather her composure. He'd completely sent her body spinning in all directions.

As she made her way to the dining room Emiliana came down the stairs. Emi stopped in front of her and giggled. "I'll come to you. Sexy."

Emi continued on to the dining room; Isabella gave her head a shake and took a few deep breaths to allow her heartbeat—and her embarrassment at getting caught—to subside.

She was almost to the dining room when the bathroom door opened and she turned to look down the hallway. Josh filled the space in a most magnificent way. He was virile, strong, crazy handsome and she thought they'd make fantastic babies together.

Dammit. Her cheeks burned bright at the thought of having babies with him. Maybe it was the thought of *making* babies with him that made her cheeks burn bright.

She waited for him to reach her, then walked in with him directly behind her. There were two places left at the table for them, side by side. He pulled out her chair, then took the seat next to her. Isabella's father immediately gave the prayer and after the subdued chorus of "Amen" the food was passed around. Considering all they'd been through, the table was rather peaceful, no harsh words, though Emi was very quiet and Mateo was still downstairs in his bedroom. Elisa had taken him a plate before dinner. Isabella planned to check on him after dinner and see if she could again appeal to him to go to the hospital. If her father granted protection to him, maybe that would make a difference.

Just as she thought it, her father announced, "I will be sending Mateo to the hospital in the morning for the medical care he needs." He looked at her. "Isi, you've done a remarkable job with him, but you yourself said he needs more than he's getting here and I believe you are correct. Mateo will no longer hold our family hostage with his shenanigans and immature behavior. I'll ask Jonny to ensure protection and that is that."

Her father then looked at Emiliana, "Emi, I am sorry. You're mother told me about your proclamation today and while I am sorry that your mother's and my decisions in the past in regards to Mateo have distressed you..." He then looked Isabella in the eyes, fidgeted in his seat and let out a deep breath. "And Isi, we did the best we thought we should do. I am deeply saddened that in doing that you girls felt as though you didn't matter. I love you both and so does your Mamá. Things will be different from this point forward."

"Thank you Papa." Emi softly replied.

Isabella looked at her father, her eyes welled with tears but she nodded her head and sent him an air kiss. Her mother, seated next to her, laid her hand on top of Isabella's and squeezed.

44

Looking at the clock on Mateo's bedside table, Josh noted that it was well past one a.m. He'd been going through the papers asking him questions about the cars and the operation. Mateo was now sleeping; the constant barrage of questions wore him out. But tomorrow, he'd be in the hospital and he might be pissed off at his father and unwilling to answer questions. Better to get it over with now.

The door opened and a stunning Isabella entered the room. She'd changed into gray sweatpants and a light pink t-shirt. Honestly, only she could wear a baggy shirt and still fill it out nicely. Her firm breasts were outlined by the fabric as it stretched across her breasts, her slim waist and hips somewhat camouflaged as it hung loosely over them.

She greeted him, but went to the bed and held her hand over Mateo's forehead, feeling for fever. She took his pulse, checked his bandages then straightened the covers over his body. Turning to him, she smiled.

"Are you ready for bed?"

He stood; it was impossible not to touch her, not to pull her close to him. He whispered close to her ear, "You coming with me?"

"Yes."

She led him by the hand to the room next door, which was Eric's room, but tonight was his.

As soon as he was inside, he closed and locked the door, tugged her hand and pulled her tightly to his body. He bent slightly and pulled her body up his; her legs instantly wrapped around his waist. He studied her as he carried her to the bed. Tonight would be the first night they actually slept together. That would be after...

He stopped at the bed and let her body slide down his. Once she hit the mattress, he kissed her lips but pulled away.

"Isi, I need a shower. Give me two minutes."

She smiled at him and his groin tightened.

He twisted and hurried to the bathroom, tugging off his shirt on the way. He didn't chance glancing at her before he stepped into the room, he'd just make this one of the quickest showers he'd ever taken. He had things to do.

He flipped on the water then pulled his gun, phone and watch off and set them on the bench at the back wall. Quickly divesting himself of his pants and briefs, Josh stepped under the hot water. A shiver ran the length of his body as the water refreshed and warmed his skin. Soaping up, he stood under the water once more when he felt soft hands exploring his body.

Swiping the water from his eyes, he saw a naked, sexy-as-sin Isabella, water sliding over her skin, her nipples tightened to points, her slim body looking more enticing than anything he could've imagined.

She pushed her body into his, the feel of her purely enticing. His hands roamed over her back, her ass, squeezing each of her globes and pulling her into his thickened cock. Her hands reached between them and grasped his length, sliding to the end and back again. The water made sliding difficult, so she reached over and poured soap on her hands. One hand on his cock, one on his balls, she massaged and pumped him expertly.

He groaned as he watched her hands, her face, her breasts as they moved and swayed before him. He waited till he was close and swiftly spun her around, her hands holding her up against the shower wall. Reaching around her, he explored Isi's body, wanting to feel every part of her. He cupped her breasts as he rubbed against her ass; his cock slid between them. He found her clit. His fingers circled, adding pressure then letting up, then adding pressure.

The sounds she made were his new favorite song. Isi whispered his name and moaned, and when she came with a gasp, he softened his manipulations and gave her a moment to enjoy the feeling before he bent his knees and positioned his cock at her entrance. She instinctively pushed herself back, presenting herself to him and he growled from deep in his chest.

He pushed himself into her, watching as his cock slowly disappeared. He pulled out and deliberately (or unhurriedly) slid back inside of her. Her warmth circled him, her body accepted him and he couldn't get enough of her, ever. His hands were everywhere on her, he didn't know what he liked touching more. He wanted to feel her everywhere. Learn her body. What she liked. As he built toward his orgasm, he grasped, her breasts and thrust into her over and over until it roared through him, his balls impossibly tight, the pain building until that final thrust and release.

"Ohh." He groaned, his hands wrapping around her and holding her close until he stopped spilling into her.

She whimpered slightly, panting, "That was hot."

He wanted to give her another orgasm—had meant to before his own overtook him. His fingers slid down her body, found her clit once more and circled around. He was still inside her, semi-hard yet, but he stroked his fingers up and down and around her clit; her breathing was ragged as her hips thrust forward into his fingers and, not wanting to slip from her body, he pulled her back tightly to him and she gasped. "Josh." His name rushed from her lips and her body jerked as her orgasm flared.

He dropped his head alongside hers and held her as tightly as he could, the warm water still flowing over their bodies, their breathing beginning to subside.

"My God, Isi, I love you."

Her arms circled his, her lips turned to his jaw. "I love you, Josh."

Sated and tired, they washed up, dried off and slid between the warm fresh sheets. He pulled her to his body, thrilled when she turned into him, her arm around his waist, her leg hooked over his. The last thought he had before he went to sleep was what they would do now. She wanted her medical clinic in Magnolia; his job was in Indiana and so was his family.

45

The first thing Isabella saw as she opened her eyes was Josh's handsome face, softened in sleep. His chest rose and fell steadily in slumber. She rolled to her other side, reached over to the nightstand and picked up her phone. 6:45 a.m.

She slipped quietly from bed, picked up her discarded clothing from the chair in the corner and dressed. She glanced back at Josh only to find him watching her.

"I'm sorry, I didn't mean to wake you."

"I don't sleep soundly Isi, it's a job hazard."

She frowned and came back to the bed to sit beside him. Smoothing her hand over his face she looked deeply into his eyes. "That's sad."

His lips tilted up at the corners, changing his face from handsome to stunning. "No it's not, it just is. I imagine Jax and Dodge are getting no sleep at all. We're all light sleepers because of the job. Being able to hear every noise is lifesaving sometimes."

"I suppose. How is Casa Martinez? Is it quiet here?"

He tucked her hair behind her ear as his eyes caressed

her. "Mateo was restless last night. He tried to move around a bit in bed, which caused him pain a few times. But he finally settled around three o'clock this morning. Otherwise, the house is pretty quiet."

Her eyes rounded. "Really? You heard him?" She shook her head. "I didn't hear a thing."

He chuckled. "It was a very long and busy day yesterday. You were exhausted."

"Not so exhausted that I didn't want to be with you."

"I'm grateful for that Angel."

"Aww. Thank you. That sounded lovely."

He shook his head. "Hasn't anyone ever called you Angel? An old boyfriend? Anyone?"

She giggled. "No. No one."

He pulled her down to him, and wrapped his arms around her body. Kissing her lips slowly but fully, his hand shifted up to her nape to hold her head in place.

"I will call you Angel from now on, because that's what you are to me. An angel, swooping into my life to make it complete."

"Is it? Complete with me?"

He swallowed and his face grew pensive. "My heart feels like it. My stomach sours when I think about what happens next because the thought of leaving you behind is like acid burning in my guts."

Tears rushed to spill over her eyes, that was, without doubt, the most romantic thing she'd ever heard.

She moved to swipe them away, but he beat her to it. Gently removing the tears from her cheeks, they continued to stare at each other.

"I feel the same way. Mamá and I were talking about it yesterday and since then, I've given a lot of thought to it. To us. To what next."

Raised voices from the room next door stopped their conversation. "No, I'll not go. Papa, he'll kill me."

Isabella jumped up and ran to the door. Glancing back at Josh, she saw him springing from bed in all his magnificent glory and running to the bathroom, where his clothes were still sitting on the bench.

She ran into Mateo's room to see her father standing alongside the bed and Mateo struggling to catch his breath.

"Papa, what's going on?" She ran to the side of the bed, hand outstretched to feel Mateo for fever, and tried to calm him. "Shh, Matty, you can't move around so much."

"Isi, he's sending me to the hospital. Tony will find me there and he'll kill me."

His words came in spurts as he tried catching his breath, small groans of pain shot through him as he expanded his lungs.

"Yes, Matty, Papa told me last night. You need X-rays, you need medicine that I don't have here. You need to make sure there are no major internal injuries. I can only listen with a stethoscope and watch for signs your body isn't functioning. I can't do the necessary tests here."

"But, if I go to get those tests, it won't matter, because I'll be dead. I'd rather die here if that's what's meant to be than by his hand."

A strong hand rested on her shoulder as her father signaled for her to move away.

She rose and stepped back. Josh entered the room and she was grateful when he held his arm out for her to slide under. As soon as she was close, he pulled her tightly to his body and stood strong for both of them.

She wrapped her arms around his waist as her father sat on the edge of Matty's bed.

"It grieves me to say this Matty. But you've twisted this family around for years with your constant troubles. It grieves me to realize how I've played a part in that by always rescuing you. And those rescues came at a cost to Isabella, Emiliana and Eric. They've had to stand by and deal with your messes while they themselves have worked hard—legitimately—and stayed out of trouble and, I won't lose another of my children because of your behavior."

She watched Mateo breathe steadily, controlling his breathing to keep from causing himself pain. His eyes welled with tears as he looked between her, Josh and her father. He asked, "What do you think, Josh? Papa seems to like you. Would you send me to the hospital if I were your son?"

Josh shook his head. "Don't drag me into this Mateo. I was happy to help find you for the family. I'll continue to work to clear you of the gun charges since I don't think you were part of that operation. But, it's not fair to ask me about the rest. I haven't had to live with all the rest."

"But..." Mateo winced as pain shot through him.

Her father stood and turned, taking in the way she and Josh held each other. His eyes landed on Josh's and they held for some time before he nodded.

"The ambulance is here to take Matty to the hospital. I'll go tell them they can come down. Isi, if you could supervise his move to the ambulance, Mamma and I would be very grateful."

"Of course, Papa."

He left the room without another word and she searched Josh's eyes. He kissed her nose and whispered. "I'm here for you and I'm not going anywhere."

She knew that meant while they moved Matty. She

prayed it also meant forever, even if it meant they'd move physically across the U.S. to anywhere else. What she knew in her heart was she wanted to be with him.

Clattering could be heard in the hallway and two men appeared in uniform, maneuvering a gurney into the room. She reluctantly moved away from Josh and began to prepare Mateo for his journey.

46

Satisfied with comparing the titles to the cars available in the lot, Josh identified all cars but two. Mateo had told him those two were still in shipping containers. He wasn't terribly excited about going back to the shipping containers to find the cars and, to be honest, there were so many containers back there, it would take a team a week. Instead, he decided to give Gaige and the police here the information he had and to then turn his focus to Carlos and his activities. He was eager to get back on American soil and he wanted to spend some time with Isabella to figure out where they went from here.

He wanted a few dates. He wanted to know more about her. What her favorite pastimes were. Did she like puppies and champagne and lobster dinners or hamburgers, kittens and beer?

His phone rang and he set the clipboard he held on the hood of a car. Jax's name appeared on the readout on his phone.

"Hey sis, how're my niece and nephew doing?"

She chuckled. "They're perfect and Dodge and I are doing great too, thanks for asking."

"I was going to get to that."

"Sure. So, work first. Hawk and Falcon found Carlos's place and they've found some shipping manifests. They also found weapons in a storage container buried in the back of the garage. We're working to match them up with their registrations but so far two of them have shown up as stolen. We should have enough evidence, once we're finished, to prove that Carlos was stuffing the cars with guns before transporting them."

"Where were they stolen from?"

"A military base in California."

"No shit?" He let that sink in. "At least now Casper will have enough to get involved, since there are stolen weapons from the military."

"Yep, we've already sent him the information and he's happy to find something to keep his ass from getting chewed."

"That's great news, Jax. Thank you."

"You bet. Now, the other reason I want to chat with you."

Here it came. He took a deep breath and held it. "I want to know about Isabella Martinez."

Slowly letting the air from his lungs he wracked his brain about where to start.

"She's gorgeous. Stunning. Crazy smart—she's a doctor. Her family is fantastic, except of course Mateo; he's definitely the black sheep problem child."

"That goes without saying."

"Right." He chuckled, "But as Mamá will say, because of this it brought Isi and I together."

Jax huffed out a breath and he heard the chair she sat

in squeak. He imagined her leaning back. "So you're together?"

Scratching his head, he turned and leaned against the car hood. "I don't know. I mean, we're together now. But, she wants to open her own clinic in Magnolia Texas. I'd have to leave GHOST to stay with her."

"You're not doing that." Her tone was one of resolve and seriousness.

"Jax..."

"Look Josh, we've lost Papa and Jake. I don't want you across the country."

"It's not fair to ask her to leave her whole family and all her dreams behind to live mine."

"She's already left her family."

"But, her dream is to open a clinic in Texas."

"We have sick people here too."

Jax's voice took on an almost panicked quality. He'd never tell her she still had hormones raging 'cause that would get his ass kicked.

He took another deep breath as he waited for Jax to calm a bit. Then he softened his voice. "Jax, I don't know what will happen. I'm here another couple of days until Travis's wedding and Isi and I have had no time to talk about us. And, it's just the damnedest thing, but we've only known each other a few days and it seems like things are moving too fast. And, well..." He took another deep breath. "I think I'm going to have to come home and really think about all of this."

"So now you're running scared?"

"No, I'm...I thought you'd be happy."

Jax cleared her throat. "Look, Josh, I remember you giving Dodge and me shit when we first got together. I remember thinking, first, that I could kick your ass if you gave me more reasons to do so. Which is likely doubtful, but I like believing I can do anything, sooo... And second, my thoughts were that I fell in love with him. That man was everything I wanted but could never dream of getting in a partner. He lets me be me. And he loves me anyway. I love looking at him. I love talking to him. And now, this may be some mommy hormones talking, but when I see him smiling at and holding our children, dammit, I fall in love all over again. There isn't a thing you could have done that would have made me walk away from him."

Swallowing the lump in his throat, he listened to the words he'd always suspected his sister felt but had never said. They didn't talk about their feelings much. Their lives were different. Always on the go, on dangerous missions, doing dangerous things and it was enough to know that Jax would lay down her life to protect him and he'd absolutely do the same for her.

"What do you think you'll do moving forward Jax?"

She laughed. "Nothing different. I love my kids. But, Mamá is here to help with them and I need to have my other purpose. I love my job too. So, I intend to keep working and Skye has said if Mamá can't watch them for some reason, she'd be happy to step in. They live close to us, she's wonderful with the kids and I'd trust her to watch them. So, Dodge and I will keep working until our bodies tell us we can't."

He nodded. "That makes me feel better sis. I wasn't sure if I'd enjoy work as much without you there."

"Damn straight you wouldn't."

He laughed out loud and it felt good. "Thanks for that. I needed a laugh. Things have been stressful."

"No doubt. So, I'll leave you with this. I won't enjoy work as much without you in it, but if your gut tells you

you have to move, I'll understand. I won't like it—at all—but I'll understand. And, you'll have to share that with Mamá."

Suddenly he felt emotional and he didn't like that at all. Squaring up his shoulders, he cleared his throat. "Okay. It's still so new and it may not even last, so, we'll have to see."

Jax laughed on the other end of the phone. "You're such a man. Stop fighting what you know to be the truth. You wouldn't even be thinking along these lines if she wasn't special. It sounds to me like you've found the one and you'd be a real dumbass to push that away because you're scared."

"I'm not scared."

"The hell you aren't."

"Look, I don't think..."

"Stop it Josh. Have you ever thought in terms of the future with anyone else?"

He looked across the parking lot, the sun was now higher in the sky, the air warming up and the glint of sunlight on the cars made it difficult to see.

"No."

"There's your answer bro. On that note, I've got to go."

The phone line silenced and he sat there a moment running all these thoughts through his head.

A voice brought him out of his pondering. "Hey bro, everything all right?"

47

Closing and zipping her medical bag, Isabella looked around the room Mateo had slept in last night to see if she had everything. Satisfied that she had picked up all her belongings and discarded all the packages from the supplies she'd used, she exited the room.

Her heart felt heavy today. Mateo had begged her father not to send him to the hospital. It was heart wrenching, and her father quickly retreated to the office afterwards, complaining that he had to fix Mateo's mistakes and clean up the business messes he'd made. It was likely that Mateo was now out of work.

Walking up the stairs to the main level, she noted how quiet the house was today. So much quieter than it had been the past couple of weeks. All the hustle and bustle of the wedding, then Mateo's latest shenanigans, had had this big ole' house jumping with people and energy. Now, it felt serene or maybe depressed. Her mother had gone to lay down; hearing Mateo's cries hurt her heart, and Emi had hidden in her room, both bothered by how hard it was to listen to Mateo and also how necessary this step had been.

She walked to the kitchen counter and lay her medical bag on the top, unzipping it again to view its contents. Taking advantage of this quiet time to make her shopping list for fresh supplies, she pulled a sheet of paper from the pad on the little desk and sat at the counter as she pulled the items from her bag and jotted down on her paper what she'd need to replenish.

Her thoughts strayed to Josh, more than once. She worried if he was safe, then chided herself for that thought. He had Diego, who was more determined than ever to get himself the help he needed and excited about the possibilities of the future.

She'd called her boss at the clinic earlier and told him she'd be out for the remainder of the week. He'd scolded her on responsibility. Patients needed her and her fellow doctors would have to pick up her slack. This made her feel even more despondent. What choice did she have? She wasn't safe yet, and while she couldn't share that information, she didn't want to be responsible for anyone else, a coworker, or a patient, being harmed if they got in the way of someone trying to attack her.

So she quietly listened as she was chastised, apologized for the delay in her return and hung up and shed a few tears. Without a doubt, this had been the most stressful week of her life.

She heaved out a heavy sigh and continued on with her task at hand. Once she'd finished up her shopping list, she packed her bag once again and took it upstairs to her bedroom here in the house. Walking past Emi's room, she saw her sister reading intently on her computer.

Quietly stepping into the room, she watched a moment, surprised Emi hadn't noticed her.

"What's so engrossing that you are glued to that computer screen?"

Emi started at her voice then turned to her. "Oh, I'm re-reading my business plan moving forward."

"Your business plan? What new enterprise are you planning for yourself?"

Emi looked her in the eye. "I want to move to the U.S. and open up my own graphic design business. I think what Papa did today was the right thing to do, Isi. It was hard, but necessary, and Matty needs to finally understand that he has to toe the line. But, for me, I want to do what you did and leave here. I want to do what *I* want to do. By staying here and working largely for Papa I feel like I'm put in a box and not able to branch out. I want to spread my wings and I don't want to be here in case Matty comes back and starts his crap all over again. You're so successful Isi and you did it by leaving first. I need to do that."

"Wow Emi, that's amazing. You'll be wonderful running your own business. You're dedicated and incredibly talented. Where would you move in the U.S.?"

Emi smiled. "I'm thinking I'd like to experience Colorado. I'm chicken to move too far north, but I do want to experience snow and fall and do some of the things they do there like snow shoeing and skiing and things like that in the mountains. My friend from college, Jessica, lives outside of Denver and she said I could live with her until I get on my feet."

"But you'll be so far away Emi."

Emiliana laughed, "Says the girl who left home and became a doctor and seldom came home anymore."

Isabella smiled. "True."

"Besides, you can hop on a plane and come see me and we'll do some hiking and fun things. And, I'll come see you. And, we'll talk on the phone, a lot. We can video conference whenever."

Isabella laughed. "You're right, we'll always be connected if we want to be."

Emi hugged her tightly and Isabella returned the hug. It felt so good. She realized it was also needed.

Pulling back she looked her sister in the eye, held both of Emi's hands in hers and said, "Emi." Taking a deep breath she smiled. "I love Josh. I am in love with Josh. It's crazy fast but when I think of going back to my life as it was before him, it leaves me feeling sad and it seems so unappealing to me now, where before it was all I wanted."

Emi grinned, so broad, so beautiful, so genuine it made her heart flutter. "I think he's perfect for you. And, he's sooo sexy too. I envy you that. He's amazing and the way he looks at you, Isi, oh it makes my heart flutter."

"Really?"

Emi giggled, "Yes, silly, really."

"Then I know what I must do."

48

He turned to see Diego walking toward him.

"Yeah. Just got off the phone with Jax."

"Oops, she chewing your ass out?"

He chuckled. "Yes and no."

Diego laughed. "Say no more."

Josh pushed himself off of the hood of the car and walked toward the car they had driven to the lot. The one still owned by Mateo.

"She did tell me that they found weapons, stolen weapons, in Carlos's home, so at least they can tie him to the stolen guns and gun running."

"That's great man. The Martinez's will be so happy they might be able to clear Mateo of those charges."

"Yeah."

He walked to the passenger side of the vehicle and opened the door. Diego slid into the driver's seat and started the SUV, cranking the air conditioning up high to get some good air flow in the vehicle.

"Heading back to Le Quemada?"

"Yeah. Then we'll be going back to Escondido. It's time we get back to Travis and Shep."

Diego pulled the SUV from the lot and nodded his head.

They drove through the town of Nuevo Laredo and Josh wondered if any of these people actually knew what was going on in the plastics factory. How many corrupt little towns were there like this all over the world? It boggled the mind and he knew from experience that the amount of dirt, drugs, trafficking, gun running and you name it other criminal activity was job security for him. He also knew he loved it every time they stopped a criminal enterprise, the bigger the better.

"I sent my application in bro. It asked what kind of problems I was having and what I felt I was still capable of doing. I'm excited about the opportunity. I'm stoked about this idea."

"How did you do last night? Any nightmares?"

"Yes. Two. They were small and I was able to calm myself down. Getting up and grabbing a drink of water helps calm my body and I can reassure myself there's no danger lurking. This week I've felt alive again, but Isi told me that could be because it's all new and fresh again and that it can flare up, so I'll continue my breathing and calming exercises and using the white noise at night to sleep until I can get proper therapy."

Josh looked over at his friend. "I'm happy for you bro. You served our country with dignity; you deserve to get the help you need."

"You deserve good things too man. A good woman."

Josh shook his head and smiled. "Yeah. I don't know, Diego."

Diego was quiet for the rest of the drive, other than

small talk about the wedding and what they should do tomorrow. They only had two more days until Travis' wedding.

Pulling his phone from his pocket, he dialed Travis' number.

"Hey, there you are. We were wondering what was going on." Travis chuckled.

"We'll be coming back tonight. I'll have Isabella with me. I promised her a night out. But the next two days, we're with you for sure."

"Sounds good. We'll make some plans."

"Looking forward to it Trav."

The line went dead and Diego glanced at him quickly. "Are you going to send Isabella back to Magnolia?"

"I don't know man. I'm all over the board on that one. She wants to live in Magnolia. I want to live in Indiana. I don't see how we get past that."

Diego swallowed but said nothing more and Josh was grateful to have the time to gather his thoughts.

Twenty minutes later they were on the picturesque driveway to the Martinez home. He remembered the first time he came down this drive in the chartered bus. His motivation then had been to help out a drunk groom and hope the bride had enough love for him that things went off without a hitch. No doubt Eric paid for it: Cecily had made him stay awake and shake hands and be the host all afternoon and evening. He looked dead on his feet by the end of it, but that was little punishment compared to her being mad and calling it all off.

The car came to a stop and he remembered the first time he saw Isabella walking from the house to come and help Eric out. Her beauty had captured him that first time.

He could only describe her as stunning. The magnetic pull was indescribably strong.

Almost as if she were summoned to him, Isabella walked out that same back door and across the stone patio to the car. His heartbeat increased as he saw the smile on her face. She was happy to see him.

Diego looked over at him. "You're a dumbass if you're going to send her home. Just sayin'."

Diego opened his door and climbed from the car, Josh did the same. Isabella's steps slowed as she looked into his face.

"Is something wrong Josh?"

"No," He lied, but her smile faded and then he felt like a big ass for lying. "Yes."

He took her hand and led her to the steps on the back patio. The shade there would keep them cooler.

He sat on the middle step and tugged her hand to sit next to him. He turned to look at her and the worry that stared back at him made his heart race.

Her voice shook when she spoke. "You're scaring me."

"Isi." He took a deep breath. "We started talking this morning and I've thought of it all day. I don't know what to do. My stomach has twisted and turned all day. I love you. But we dream of being in different places. I don't know how to get past that. My job, which is a huge part of my life, and my family, are in Indiana. I don't have options to work, doing what I do, anywhere else. And, I can't ask you to give up your dream of Magnolia and your own clinic."

A tear fell from her right eye and with a shaking finger, he reached over and swiped it away.

49

Staring into those gorgeous brown eyes, those impossibly thick lashes, his tanned skin and those delicious full lips, she knew exactly what she wanted.

"So, you'll give me up to go back home?"

"I don't want..." His voice hitched and she watched his Adam's apple as he swallowed repeatedly. At least it was hard for him. But she was going to make him say it. He cleared his throat. "I don't want to go home without you. But I can't ask..." He took a deep breath and held it for ten or more seconds before letting it out slowly.

"I love what I do for a living. I'm bringing down criminals and I'm helping to save people. We all are. I work with men and women who are like my own blood family and I also work with my blood family. Jax is still working and so is Dodge and they've created two gorgeous little humans that I want to watch grow up. My family is very close. You'd fit right in. You'd love them and they'll love you. Not even a question. But..."

She took a deep breath and reached for his hands. She

held them both in her own and squeezed. Looking at their hands together, each holding on to the other, she knew that's what they needed to do.

"See how our hands know what we have to do? They're holding on tightly to the other. When things are getting hard, they're seeking each other as a lifeline to hold on tight. That's what we have to do. We have to hold on tight."

She squeezed his hands again. "Josh Masters, I told you I love you and I meant it. I love you more right now than I loved you this morning. I'll love you tomorrow more than I love you right now. And that's how it will be every day until the day we die. I can be a doctor anywhere. Any city. Any town. Any country. Right now, I choose Lynyrd Station, Indiana."

A sob exploded from his chest and he easily pulled her into his lap and folded his arms around her tightly as her arms wrapped around his shoulders. She sobbed with him as they held each other. Her body shook because she knew this was right and she was scared and excited and nervous and you name it, she was. But she could be a doctor anywhere.

He pulled back and kissed her lips. "Are you sure Isi? You have to be sure."

"I am sure. I'm absolutely sure. Magnolia was a dream because it's what I knew. But, today Emi said she's moving to Colorado because she wants to be free to follow her dreams. You are my dream, Josh."

He kissed her lips again, and again, and again. "Isabella Martinez, you are my dream. You are absolutely my dream come true."

They sat holding each other quietly for a while.

"Should we get ready to go back to Escondido or are we staying here tonight?"

"Yes, I'd like to go back. I've ignored Travis and Shep for far too long."

"Oh my God, I am so sorry. I've barely given them thought during all of this. Maybe you should go back without me. I'll go to Magnolia and make arrangements to move and, wait, do you want me to move right away? Should I wait for a while?"

He laughed and when he laughed he was without a doubt the sexiest man in the world. No comparison to be made. Flat out sexiest man in the world.

"Yes, I'd love for you to come home with me right away, but is that even possible? What do you need to do? Do you have a house to sell?"

She laughed too. It was the relieved laugh of someone who had pent up stress and negative energy for far too long and it felt wonderful to let it out of her body.

"Okay, how about this? Let's go back to Escondido. I'll work out transferring my medical license and find out what must be done for that, put my condo on the market, and figure out what else has to be done while you're out playing with your friends."

Josh sobered a moment, "Well, first I have to arrange security for you, because we still have Tony to deal with. So, let's do this. We'll go back to Escondido and on the way I'll call Gaige and Jax and see what they can arrange for security. They can vet them and get someone reliable. Only after we have that will I go outside and play with my friends."

She leaned in and kissed his lips. Softer this time. Less tension. More purposeful. His lips molded to hers. His hands smoothed across her back and slid into her hair holding her head gently in place.

When they pulled apart he whispered, "I love you, Isabella. I love you with my whole heart."

The closing of the back door had them turning around to see her parents standing on the patio smiling at them.

"That is a beautiful site to see, querida." Her mother said.

Isabella stood from Josh's lap, then he stood as well, holding her hand they met her parents.

"Mamá and Papa, I'm not sure how much you heard, but I'm moving to Indiana to be with Josh."

Her mother pulled her in to a soft warm motherly hug and she fought the tears that once again threatened to fall.

"I'm so happy, Isi. You two are good together. I can see the love."

"Thank you, Mamá."

She looked over at her father and he held his arms to pull her into a warm hug. "It's right."

She nodded and squeezed her father.

When she stepped back, she saw that her mother was hugging Josh. Then her father looked at Josh and said, "We'll have a private word now."

Her father walked into the house; Josh grinned at her and followed her father.

50

Ivan walked to his office and Josh stepped inside.

"Close the door please."

Nervous that this was not going to be a good conversation, he closed the door. When he turned around, Ivan had walked to a wall of shelves and opened a carved wooden box about the size of a shoe box on the center shelf.

With something in his hand, motioned to the chairs sitting across from his desk and said, "Take a seat."

Josh did as he was told, a heaviness settling in his chest.

"I'll get to the point. What are your intentions with Isabella? She's special. Not only is she beautiful outside, as you can see, she's beautiful inside. She's smart and she cares for people. As her father, I want to protect her as much as I can. So, at the risk of repeating myself, what are your intentions with Isabella?"

Josh sat forward in the leather wing back chair he sat in. He looked Ivan directly in the eye and stated, "I hope to marry her."

"You hope?"

"She has to say yes."

Ivan nodded his head; the salt and pepper hair on this man, still full and neatly trimmed, only added to his impressive stature. Easily six feet tall, he remained slim and always stood tall and straight.

"That's true."

Ivan reached forward and lay a small black velvet box on the desk. "This ring belonged to my mother. She and my father owned this house before Bianca and I took it over. She asked me to save it for Isi and to give it to her future husband only if I thought he was worthy. If you are intending to marry my daughter, I give this ring to you for her. My request is that when Isi is no longer, that one of your children or grandchildren will then have the honor of wearing this ring."

Josh reached forward and swallowed. Holding the box in his shaking hands, he lifted the lid and his eyes rounded at the ring that lay inside. It was easily a three-carat diamond ring with smaller diamonds on either side and intricate scrolling in the yellow gold band. He didn't know much about diamonds, other than the pink one Jax wore and the significance of it, but he knew this was special.

His eyes lifted to meet Ivan's. "Does Isi know about this ring?"

"Yes. But, she doesn't know it's for her. None of the children knew, they just knew it would be given to one of them one day."

Josh swallowed. "Does she want it?"

Ivan sat back in his big leather chair. "Yes, she does. You don't like it?"

"It's beautiful. I just wanted to make sure it was something that Isi wanted before I place it on her finger."

"Well, as you've said, she has to say yes first."

"Right."

Ivan stood and so did Josh. He put the ring in his front right pocket, then reached across the desk with his hand out to shake Ivan's hand.

"Thank you sir. I wanted to ask her to marry me earlier but I didn't have a ring to give her."

"Now you do."

Josh nodded and left the office. He followed the murmur of voices to the patio, where Isabella, Bianca, Emiliana and Diego all sat talking and drinking iced tea.

They all looked up at him and he nodded in greeting.

"Isi, may I speak with you?"

She looked scared again; her smile faded as she stood. "Sure."

Her eyes darted behind him to where Ivan now stood, then back to him.

He took her hand and slowly led her off the patio and toward the edge of the driveway. There he stopped and turned to face her.

"The first time I came to this house I was sitting in a bus right there." He pointed to the left. "You came out of the house and walked to this spot right here as I helped Eric off the bus. The first time I laid eyes on you was on this spot right here." He looked at the ground. "At that very moment in time, it was as if everything else faded to dark and all I could see was you. It was as if you had a light from heaven shining on you and God was telling me, "Josh, this is her, this is your future, your life. Do you remember that Isi? The first time we saw each other?"

"Yes I do. I will always remember it."

"Then it is fitting that right here on this spot..." He knelt on one knee and pulled the ring from his pocket. "Isabella Martinez, will you be my wife? Will you be my life?"

Tears spilled as she nodded her gorgeous head. "Yes," she whispered finally. He opened the lid on the box and she sobbed.

"Abuela's ring?"

"Yes."

He pulled it from the box with shaking fingers and held her left hand as he slowly slipped the ring on her ring finger. The stunning diamond looked perfect on her hand. "It's a perfect fit. It was meant to be for you Isi."

She stared at it as he stood, then threw herself into his arms and laughed and sobbed and squeezed him tightly.

He held her close, enjoying the way she felt in this moment and looking forward to all the future moments they'd share together.

She pulled her head back but kept her arms tightly wrapped around his neck. Her lips molded to his, softly and sweetly, their tongues tasting and sliding along each other.

Applause from the patio had them both looking and he laughed. "I'd forgotten they were watching us."

Isi giggled, "Me too."

He set her gently on the ground and took her left hand in his and walked to the patio as his new family congratulated them on their future.

Josh's phone rang; Gaige's name appeared on his phone. He stepped away from the raucous congratulations.

"Masters."

"Josh, I just wanted to let you know Mexican authorities captured Tony Morales. He's in custody and they are now disassembling his enterprise. Even better news, he had part of his enterprise in the U.S. so Casper is working on what he can from here. That doesn't mean Mateo is completely cleared, but it does mean the Martinez family is not in any further danger."

"That's fantastic, Gaige, thank you. I'll let them know and you're right, that is good news."

51

She took a deep breath as the GHOST plane landed. Josh leaned over and took her hand in his.

"They are going to love you. I promise."

"It's still nerve-racking meeting everyone at once."

"I met your whole family at once."

She laughed. "I know but it's not the same."

He laughed with her. "True."

The plane came to a halt near the hangar and Josh unbuckled his seatbelt. She followed his lead and waited to see when he stood up.

The hatch opened after a few moments and the curtain between the cabin and the cockpit and exit door opened. Gavin, their pilot, smiled at them and nodded.

"Welcome home Mr. Masters, Ms. Martinez."

She smiled at Gavin, and Josh stood and took her hand. As they passed the luggage area, he stopped and unstrapped their luggage, and pulled her two suitcases from the holding area. He slung his bag over his shoulder than nodded to her.

"You go ahead of me Isi."

"I can take one of my bags Josh."

He just laughed and stood still.

She started down the steps.

"Thanks Gavin." Josh said as they passed him.

After disembarking, Josh led them through the hangar. A large black SUV sat alongside the garage door on the other side of the building.

"This is the Beast. She's exactly what her name indicates."

He set the suitcases on the ground behind the Beast, opened the passenger door for her and she climbed in. He then loaded their luggage into the back while she stared in amazement at all the gadgets and buttons on the dash.

Josh climbed into the driver's seat and chuckled. "Amazing, right?"

"Yes."

He tapped a button on the visor and the garage door opened. He pushed a button on the dash and the Beast started. Soon they were rolling out of the hangar.

"How did the Beast get to the hangar? Did Gavin bring it?"

"No, a couple of the team members likely brought it and left it here a while ago. We're always shuttling vehicles to and from this airport for our team members. Sometimes, if we bring our personal vehicles, we'll just leave them here, but I was gone for a few days and we don't want that space taken in the hangar. If the team needed to park there, like Hawk and Falcon did when they came down to Texas, they'd park one of their vehicles in here."

"You are all a well-oiled machine."

"We are. Wait till you see the compound."

She giggled. "Oh the images that conjures."

He chuckled. "Just wait."

They drove through the town and she gawked at the quaint buildings and happy looking storefronts as they passed by. The stores had planters out front which added color and softness along the street. The older buildings were well kept and all the storefronts were open.

"This is a cute town."

He chuckled. "It is. It's very nice here. Small town, welcoming and friendly."

Josh continued driving about a half mile after the town came to an end. Turning into a driveway with gates across the middle, he tapped a button and the gates rolled open. There was construction on both sides of the house, which was a stunning Southern-style mansion complete with a large rounded portico and columns in the front.

"Wow, what is this?"

"This, Angel, is the compound."

"No way."

He chuckled and she tried taking in all there was to see. "What is all the construction?"

He stopped the Beast as the gates rolled closed behind them. Pointing to the right he said, "Wyatt and Yvette are building a new house right there. There will be an underground tunnel connecting their house to the compound here."

Pointing toward the back, he said, "You can't really see it completely, but Axel, Bridget and Aidyn will be living there. I'll give you a tour. Not sure about the tunnel yet, but as you can see, we have a large fence around the whole compound. Gaige has managed to negotiate with the neighbors to buy out their homes so we can continue to grow and yet, in an emergency, still be close enough when needed. When we were all single, it was convenient to stay here. We'll be here for a while, but will have to talk about what we want to do in the future. Gaige and Sophie have a baby, Tate, and no doubt will have more, so they'll need the space, not that they are kicking us out, but as we each have our own families, it makes sense for us to move out and leave room for them and for future single operatives."

She looked to the left. "What's going on over there?"

He smiled. "That is for future expansion."

She laughed and looked around at the area. "Where does Jax live?"

He pushed a button and a garage door to the far right opened. As he drove toward the door he said, "Jax, Dodge, Maya and Myles live about a mile out of town at the base of a mountain, Lynyrd Station on the Hill; Ford owns it. Ford, Megan and Shelby live at the top of Lynyrd Station on the Hill, and Lincoln and Skye live at the base on the other side from Dodge and Jax. "

"Okay. Wow."

They began descending to below ground and her eyes rounded. "Holy cow."

He laughed. "I should have warned you but I wanted to see your surprise. So, our garage is two levels below ground. It's secure and private."

"I'm dumbfounded."

He laughed. "I'm enjoying myself watching your reaction. I'm also getting the feeling that you thought you were giving up a gorgeous little town to come and live on a military-type compound without color or luxury."

She looked over at him and smiled. "I did."

He chuckled and she was torn between staring at him and looking around.

The garage was full and he chuckled. "Looks like the whole gang is here to meet you."

She took a deep breath and let it out slowly. When Josh had met her family, he didn't care if they liked him. But, she really wanted these men and women to like her. It helped a bit that she'd already met Hawk and Falcon but from the stories she'd heard about Jax, and knowing Josh and Jax were so close, she really hoped they could be great friends.

Josh parked the Beast at the back of the garage, backing it in so it was ready to go. He got out and walked around the Beast to her door. Opening it for her, he reached in and took her hand. Once she'd stepped down, he kissed her lips softly and sweetly and whispered, "Welcome home."

Opening the hatch, Josh pulled their bags from the back, slinging his over his shoulder, he lifted the handles on her bags and she took one, he took the other, then, holding her hand, he led her to an elevator.

Waving a card in front of a panel he smiled. "So, this is the lowest level we have here. The level directly above us is our main operations. We have a conference room which is also our computer lab. We have a shooting range, workout room, and a medical clinic on site."

"You have a doctor here?"

"We do now." He squeezed her hand. "Wyatt is our team medic and is able to do most of the patch work we need, especially in a pinch in the field. But he'll be the first to tell you, he's no doctor. He'll likely be relieved to have someone else to bounce medical questions off."

"Wow, okay."

They stepped into the elevator, and he pushed the button that had a 2 on it.

"For now, I'll take you upstairs to our room, we can drop our bags and then we'll go down to the dining room, where it's likely everyone is."

"Okay."

The elevator rose through the building and her heart raced. This was all beginning to feel very real. They'd sort of lived a fairy tale to this point. Well, if a fairy tale included stealing, kidnapping, shooting, and all the other intrigue.

The doors quietly slid open and they stepped out into a lovely hallway with a multitude of doors. Josh turned them right and they stepped across the hall to the second door. He pointed to the door directly across from the elevator as they passed. "That was Jax's room when she lived here."

He then pulled his key card out and waved it in front of the second door. "This is our room."

He pushed the door open and stepped aside for her to enter first. She jumped when she saw a gorgeous woman sitting on Josh's bed.

52

Josh stepped in behind Isi to find Jax staring at them. He laughed and quickly met his sister as she jumped at him. He picked her up and spun her around as they hugged fiercely.

"Isi, this is Jax." He set Jax on the floor and reached out for Isabella. "Jax, this is my future wife, Isabella Martinez."

Jax smiled brightly at Isabella, then hugged her.

"It's very nice to meet you, Isabella."

Jax stepped aside then and gestured at the sofa, which was partially hidden by the open door. "This is my husband, Dodge Sager."

Dodge stood and walked forward. "How are you doing, Isabella?"

Isabella smiled as she looked between Jax and Dodge, then Dodge bent and hugged her.

Josh watched as Isabella hugged Dodge. He pulled her into the side of his body and looked at his sister and brother-in-law.

"What are you two doing in my room?"

Jax laughed. "I can still get in if I want and, I wanted to meet Isabella without all the others around because I thought she might be nervous."

Isi smiled. "I am nervous. Thank you for thinking of me."

"Where are my niece and nephew?"

"Next door. Mamá is watching them. She's likely going crazy waiting to meet her newest daughter and by the looks of you, Isabella, and don't take this the wrong way, but you are much more feminine than I am, so Mamá will be thrilled."

Typical Jax attire was tactical pants, shirts and boots, which she wore again today. Isabella wore a light, soft pink sweater and white dress slacks. All feminine and pretty. He couldn't have been prouder.

Isi's cheeks turned a beautiful shade of blush and Josh laughed. "You'll soon find out that Jax and Mamá argue all the time about Jax being more comfortable in tactical attire. Even at their wedding the arguments were non-stop. Jax won, in the end, because she had a gorgeous wedding gown, but she wore..." he looked at Jax's boots, "those."

Isabella laughed and so did Jax.

Dodge leaned down and kissed Jax's lips sweetly. "She's her own woman for certain, and it's one of the things I love most about her."

Josh beamed at his sister and her husband. They were perfectly matched, and he loved that she'd found the one for her.

Jax winked at Dodge then turned to them and smiled. "Okay, let's go put Mamá out of her misery." She walked out of the room, Dodge close behind.

Josh looked down at Isi. "Not so bad, right?"

Isi smiled. "Not bad at all. I think I already love her."

Taking her hand, he pulled her behind Jax and Dodge.

The instant Jax opened the door, she exclaimed, "Mamá, you changed her clothes? Why did you do that?"

"Because, she is precious in her frills. You dress her like a member of GHOST."

"I do not, but so what if I do."

Josh leaned down. "See?"

Isabella laughed. "Oh my God."

She stepped into the room. There stood his mother, who rushed to him and wrapped him in a hug. Though she was much smaller, his mamá's hugs always made him feel special.

He stepped back and pulled Isi forward. "Mamá, this is Isabella. Isi, my Mamá, Pilar."

His mother smiled her brightest smile, "Oh, Isabella, you are so beautiful. I am so happy to meet you."

She wrapped Isabella in a hug and Isi hugged her right back. His heart felt full. This was his family and though he knew Isi's family was also important to her and they'd absolutely stay in close contact and visit them often, the love he felt right now—that she was willing to move here with him—it meant more than anything else could.

When his mother stood back, she looked at Isi's face, then her clothing, and then turned to Jax. "Jacqueline, this is how…"

"Nope. Don't say it, Mamá. You now have a girly daughter you can fuss over."

Jax winked at Isabella. "This is going to work out great. But I feel for you—she's going to want the whole big wedding. Catholic wedding at Saint Francis, which our families and we want, too, but she may try to get the

Bishop to perform the Mass. The frills, oh, Lord, I feel for you."

His mother tsked and mumbled the Bishop would be too busy, and Jax laughed. "See?"

Jax walked over to the bed and scooped up one of the babies; Dodge picked up the other and brought them over. Dodge beamed down at his son then looked at Isabella.

"This is Myles and Maya."

Isabella smiled brightly as she looked at the babies; both of them had grown since he'd been gone, and he was immediately sorry he'd missed that. Jax handed him Maya. Her thick, dark hair stood out against the pink headband his mother had placed on her head, the pink, frilly dress a beautiful contrast to her soft olive skin.

"Your children are absolutely gorgeous." Isabella softly said. Dodge handed Myles over to her and Isi smiled down at the little bundle in her arms and Josh saw their future. They were going to have a bunch of these.

They visited for a while until Maya started crying. Jax took her from Josh's arms. "It's feeding time. You two go downstairs. Everyone is excited to meet you. They're all in the dining room. We'll come down once we have these two fed."

Josh turned to Isi. "Ready?"

"Yes." She smiled brightly and he couldn't wait to show her off.

Then she turned to Jax and Dodge and said, "Thank you for meeting us up here. I was very nervous to meet you all, especially Josh's family."

Jax just smiled. "I figured. You'll be fine with this group. No prima donnas here. Our work lives are dramatic enough; here, we chill."

Dodge hinted to Josh, "Go down the stairs."

His brows furrowed but he nodded. Leading Isi to the door they walked out the door and he led her past the elevator and to the staircase. "This is the grand staircase..."

The foyer below was festively decorated in welcome banners, flowers, balloons and as they appeared at the top of the stairs a chorus of voices yelled, "Welcome home."

***

Mr. & Mrs. Ivan Martinez, together with Ms. Pillar Masters invite you to the wedding of their children, Isabella Martinez and Joshua Masters.

To attend the wedding go here - https://dl.bookfunnel.com/umowe8i5pu

***

Diego is about to embark on a whole new life. Join him as he meets Shelby, Callie and Anders in **Saving Shelby, RAPTOR Book One**

https://books2read.com/u/bPy8Kr

ENJOY THIS BOOK? YOU CAN MAKE A BIG DIFFERENCE

Reviews are the most powerful tools in my arsenal when it comes to getting attention for my books. As much as I'd like to, I don't have the financial muscle of a New York publisher. I can't take out full page ads in the newspaper or put posters on the subway.

(Not yet, anyway.)

But I do have something much more powerful and effective than that, and it's something that those big publishers would die to get their hands on.

A committed and loyal bunch of readers.

Honest reviews of my books help bring them to the attention of other readers.

If you've enjoyed this book I would be so grateful to you if you could spend just five minutes leaving a review (it can be as short as you like) on the book's vendor page. You can jump right to the page of your choice by clicking below.

Thank you so much - Leave your review now.

ALSO BY PJ FIALA

You can find all of my books at https://pjfiala.com/books

Romantic Suspense

Rolling Thunder Series

Moving to Love, Book 1

Moving to Hope, Book 2

Moving to Forever, Book 3

Moving to Desire, Book 4

Moving to You, Book 5

Moving On, Book 6

Rolling Thunder Boxset 1, Books 1-3

Rolling Thunder Boxset 2, Books 4-6

Military Romantic Suspense

Second Chances Series

Designing Samantha's Love, Book 1

Securing Kiera's Love, Book 2

Bluegrass Security Series

Heart Thief, Book One

Finish Line, Book Two

Lethal Love, Book Three

Wrenched Fate, Book Four

Lynyrd Station Protectors - Security

Finding His Fire Book One

Finding His Mark Book Two

Finding His Jewel Book Three

Finding His Match Book Four

Lynyrd Station Protectors - Special Ops

Defending Keirnan, GHOST Book One

Defending Sophie, GHOST Book Two

Defending Roxanne, GHOST Book Three

Defending Yvette, GHOST Book Four

Defending Bridget, GHOST Book Five

Defending Isabella, GHOST Book Six

GHOST Box Set One (Books 1-3)

GHOST Box Set Two (Books 4-6)

Lynyrd Station Protectors - Trafficking

RAPTOR Rising - Prequel

Saving Shelby, RAPTOR Book One

Holding Hadleigh, RAPTOR Book Two

Craving Charlesia, RAPTOR Book Three

Promising Piper, RAPTOR Book Four

Missing Mia, RAPTOR Book Five

Believing Becca, RAPTOR Book Six

Keeping Kori, RAPTOR Book Seven

Healing Hope, RAPTOR Book Eight

Engaging Emersyn, RAPTOR Book Nine

RAPTOR Box Set 1

RAPTOR Box Set 2

RAPTOR Box Set 3

GHOST Legacy (Next generation)

Finding Lara, Book One

Saving Elena, Book Two

Rescuing Kenna, Book Three

Protecting Everleigh, Book Four

Guarding Adelaide, Book Five

Shielding Maya, Book Six

MEET PJ

Writing has been a desire my whole life. Once I found the courage to write, life changed for me in the most profound way. Bringing stories to readers that I'd enjoy reading and creating characters that are flawed, but lovable is such a joy.

When not writing, I'm with my family doing something fun. My husband, Gene, and I are bikers and enjoy riding to new locations, meeting new people and generally enjoying this fabulous country we live in.

I come from a family of veterans. My grandfather, father, brother, two sons, and one daughter-in-law are all veterans. Needless to say, I am proud to be an American and proud of the service my amazing family has given.

My online home is https://www.pjfiala.com.
You can connect with me on Facebook at https://www.facebook.com/PJFialaI,
and
Instagram at https://www.Instagram.com/PJFiala.
If you prefer to email, go ahead, I'll respond - pjfiala@pjfiala.com.

COPYRIGHT

Copyright © 2021 by PJ Fiala

All rights reserved. This book or any portion thereof may not be reproduced or used in any manner whatsoever without the express written permission of the publisher except for the use of brief quotations in a book review.

Publisher's note: This is a work of fiction. Names, characters, places, and incidents either are the product of the author's imagination or are used fictitiously. Any resemblance to actual events, locales, or persons, living or dead, is entirely coincidental.

Printed in the United States of America

First published 2021

Fiala, PJ

DEFENDING ISABELLA / PJ Fiala

p. cm.

1. Romance—Fiction. 2. Romance—Suspense. 3. Romance - Military

I. Title – DEFENDING ISABELLA

ISBN: 978-1-942618-57-7

www.ingramcontent.com/pod-product-compliance
Lightning Source LLC
Chambersburg PA
CBHW051011180726
48291CB00006B/2057